MW01615262

An Indigo T

Lynx on Fire

Merri Halma

By Merri Halma

Follow the cat tracks

Cover art by Cynthia Martinez

ISBN 13: 978-0-578-51694-3

10: 0-578-51694-2

This is work of fiction. All characters are fictious.

Dedicated to Clarence Halma

1999 to 2017
We miss you.

Acknowledgements

Lynx has a story to tell. The character was at first inspired by our cat, Demon, whom I would have named Lynx, if I had met him first. My oldest stepdaughter brought Demon to our home when she and her sister came to stay with us full time. Demon lived up to his name because he would claw, scratch and bite us whenever we least expected it. He tried to beat up Clarence, but soon Clarence let him know who the boss was in the house. But Demon was the bully, and after a while, he settled down to become a mellow cat who learned to accept us and not lash out when we weren't expecting it.

I had to write my cats into my stories. Originally, I expected Clarence's role to be more involved, but the stories always write themselves, and often the characters that need to be in the forefront, push out those that don't have a solid role.

My werecat Lynx has evolved from the first time he has appeared. He is loved, I hope, by all my fans and those who see him as more mischievous than demon. Though, he will confront that part of his nature

I want to thank Dawn Schuldenfrei for putting up with my moods as we work together. Jeanette Andersen for being a friend. Mike Hanson of the UPS Store #3067 for assisting me with graphic set up and formatting. Thank you, Steve Wilhelm for editing. You are missed in the Treasure Valley Author's meetings.

And thank you to Cynthia Martinez for all her beautiful covers she has done for me. I'm sorry to say Lynx on Fire will be her last book cover. I wish her good luck in her other pursuits.

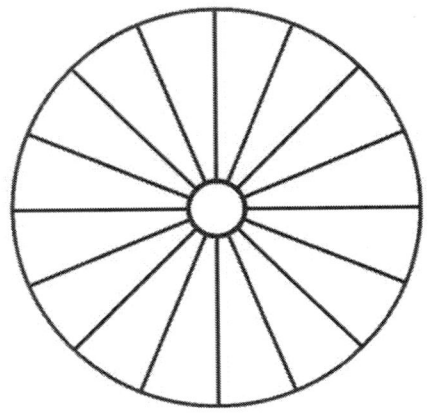

We go by many names
We surround you,
Inside,
Outside
Genderless
Species less
Shifting forms
Hear our voices deep inside you, whispering
The Still, small voice
All Paths lead to us.
In this world,
We are All There Is
The Teachings of Albagoth

Prologue

Lynx, the grey and black striped werecat, dragged his ragged body through the Senilona desert. The villagers from Kent Kingdom had chased him out with broom sticks, torches and battle axes, threatening to set him on fire after they arrested his friend and caregiver, Alchemist Blacksmith Tarrier, accusing him of being a traitor to the Crown. Lynx paused, his long, usually fluffy, elegant tail drooped down, looking ragged and fatigued. He lifted his paws, flexing his four toes and new opposable toe on both front paws. He snapped each opposable toe against the first toe. He called his opposable toes thumbs.

A few of the men grew near, positioning their torches close to his hind quarters as he ran. Lynx felt the fire lick his fur and skin. Crying out, his mind switched to kitten hood, engulfed in flames as boys laughed and hooted as they retreated away from the alleyway.

"One more demon cat torched. Let's find another," he heard them say.

Lynx's dream observer knew that Kentese villagers didn't say that. That memory belonged to another time, long forgotten and buried. The dream observer withdrew from the scene.

Chapter 1

The flames leaped into the air, snapping, crackling and popping. Lynx and Geoffrey paced the outskirts of the bonfire, watching Xander, Sarah and other kids from the junior class throw more oak, willow and birch logs on to it. Milo led the cheer squad to build the school spirit in their homecoming football game the next night.

Something about the flames frightened, yet mesmerized Lynx. He slowly approached the bonfire, with a mixture of curiosity and repulsion – spellbound by the flames licking up to the sky, cackling and laughing. At the same time, other flames were jetting out to the sides as if they were trying to pull in those who stood too close. Drawing him in – losing control of his large paws. Memories he had closed away a long time ago held him captive.

"You're nothing, Runt! Mamma hasn't got enough milk for you! Better run along and find your own food!" his older werecub brother pushed him toward the entrance of their nest.

"Ro-ar!" Runt replied, trying to snarl and hiss at his brother. His brother laughed.

"You can't even roar or talk! You're defective!"

Those words stabbed Runt. He flattened his ears against his head, tears welling up behind his golden eyes. He whimpered as he tried to run off deeper into the cave that was their nest, but his other brothers and sisters barred his way. They knocked him back and then forced him to back-step to the oldest brother who was waiting to back paw him into the wall of the hard rocks. Runt hit it hard, knocking the wind out of him and the stone cut deep into his side. Sliding to the floor, he whimpered. Stunned and aching, he couldn't move for several minutes.

Runt took a deep breath and felt his spirit rise from his body as he exhaled. He looked down on his weremates, observing their actions and the words.

"Leave now, Runt! You're not wanted here! No one loves you!" When Runt didn't move, he went over and kicked the small werecub hard. "I said leave! Get up and get out of here before Mamma and Dadpa get back!"

The next oldest sister came up, "Claude, I think you killed the little, annoying Runt. He isn't moving. C'mon, leave it alone."

"He would go and die like that! It takes the fun out of pushing it around. Come on, get up! Move, you yellow liver toad!"

"What's going on here, Claude!" said their Mamma and Dadpa from behind, startling the oldest werecub.

"Um, nothing," he said, turning around facing his parents, trying to hide the unconscious, youngest werecub.

"What's behind your back?" Dadpa demanded.

"Nothing." Claude shook his head back and forth.

"If it is nothing, then move out of the way."

Slowly, Claude moved, to show his parents the unconscious werecub.

"My baby!" Mamma sobbed, running up the unconscious Runt. Gently, she picked him up by the scuff of the neck and carried him to a small fire deep inside the cave where the other werepride were. The healer came towards her, offering prayers and herbs they stole from the Ohana people in the village. They didn't willingly give them the healing herbs.

Runt's spirit drifted out of the cave, not sure what to do. Sensing food, he drifted deep into the forest to watch the other animals of this world. He was too young to explore on his own. All his five weremates were old enough, but Claude, being the oldest by twelve hours, saw himself as the boss. There were ten other cubs that came after Claude. Runt was the youngest. Being only few months old now, he didn't know what to do. He should be talking, but somehow, he wasn't learning to form the words or sounds yet. Werecats shift into other shapes and images. But his Dadpa encouraged them not to shift yet. That comes when they're older – maybe six months or a year-old. Runt peered down from above, watching as his parents dragged his lifeless form towards the center fire, keeping the other members of their den warm. He became aware of other animals and beings stirring outside. He headed towards them.

There was another fire deep in the woods. Runt drifted to it. A large bear family sat around it, eating fish, nuts and berries. Runt spotted Ohanaians, beings that walked on two-legs and had no hair except on their heads. They were funny looking animals. These beings were not moving, too. It looked like they had been mauled by the bears. A small cub looked up, spotted Runt's spirit and pointed.

"Look, Dadpa, there is a werecub's ghost. We got to send it over the hill to the land of the All That Is!"

His dadpa slapped him, "There is no such thing as the All That Is! Ohanaians believe that foolishness. We are the gods of this world and the next!"

Runt felt a gentle pull and then abruptly his spirit soared back to his body. He woke, crying in pain and anger.

"Come back, my little Runt," his mamma cooed. "It isn't your time yet."

"Lynx, snap out of it!" Geoffrey punched him.

Lynx shook his head. "Where am I?" he looked around, heard the cheerleaders and crowd still chanting and saw Milo doing his series of flips, roundups and spins to the joy of the crowd, getting them pumped for the big game the next night.

"Oh, we're still at the bonfire," Lynx sighed.

"Come follow me. This smoke is messing up my senses and sinuses," Geoffrey led Lynx away from the fire. Once they got to a clearing, the griffin, with his glamour of an eight-foot-tall Great Dane, turned around to face his friend, Lynx, who looked like a larger than normal Maine Coon, "What were you thinking?"

"What do you mean?" Lynx asked, glancing around, noticing several groups of teens strolling around, chatting, giggling and teasing each other. Some held cups of steaming drink Lynx guessed was hot chocolate or coffee.

"You kept getting closer and closer to that fire. I was scared you would walk right into it. It was like you were on autopilot."

Lynx wagged his head to one side and sighed, shrugging his shoulders. "I don't know. That fire brought back strange memories of when I was a cub. Not sure." His voice trailed off.

"Not sure of what?"

Hearing some giggling close by, Geoffrey and Lynx turned to see two teen girls and two teen boys standing by them, oohing and awing. Geoffrey spoke, "What's up?" But the kids heard, "Woof – woof," in a deep baritone voice.

"What a big doggie." the girls cooed. "Who do you belong to? Are you lost?"

"Look at the size of those paws!" one of the guys uttered.

"They look like lion paws!" the second guy said.

"I don't belong to anyone!" Geoffrey growled. But it came out as a snarl. The teens backed up. Lynx came forward, his tall ears standing up and the tufts on top of them waved in the light breeze.

"Leave my friend alone!" Lynx snapped. But it came out more like a hiss.

"If I didn't know better, I'd say that cat was defending his friend." Said the second boy.

"Hey, it did appear like those two were conversing," said one of the girls.

"Don't be silly, Maggie. Animals can't talk to each other!"

"Wanna bet?" Xander stepped up from behind them. The four teens looked at him.

"How would you know, Veh?" The two boys sneered.

"These two live with me," Xander put his hand out, Geoffrey and Lynx walked up to him, lowered their heads and rubbed against it, mimicking pets. "These two are pretty special beings and don't see themselves as animals. They are also best friends with each other.'"The four teens laughed. "Milo says you've changed. But you're as weird as those stories that Digger Martin writes about on the Exploring with Indigo Travelers website. I don't think you will ever change, Veh. You will always be strange."

They walked off, talking about the large paws that Geoffrey and Lynx had.

Geoffrey and Lynx snarled, glaring at the four teens' backs.

"Forget them," Xander said. "We're almost done here and can go home. The fire department will help us put the bon fire out."

One of the girls came back, "Excuse me, Xander," she said softly. He turned.

"Yes, Betty?" he answered her.

"Sorry for how the guys treated you. I just was admiring how large your pets are. I've never seen a Great Dane or cat as large as them," she said.

"They aren't a normal dog and cat."

"What made them grow so big?"

"Maybe it's because I'm a werecat that can shift into any shape I want to be and Geoffrey is actually a griffin," Lynx sneered.

Betty heard Lynx hiss and spit. She jumped back.

"Um, why is he so upset?"

"Lynx be good. She's trying to make friends," Xander admonished.

"Harrumph!"

"Lynx!"

"Rrrrawr!"

"I'll deal with you later!"

"Like that will ever happen! Wait till I tell your mom," Lynx fired.

Xander shot him an angry look. "Act like a tame house cat," he whispered.

"I'm not a normal housecat, Xander! Besides, she's listening to us."

Xander looked up to the heavens, *Albagoth, what am I ever going to do with this werecat?*

"That's cute how you talk to your pets," Betty giggled. "You carry on a conversation with him like you understand his snarls and meows."

"I do understand him. That's one of my gifts as an Indigo teen. Look, Betty, my animals grew so big because they're loved a lot and because they're special. Haven't you heard of Clifford the Big Red Dog?"

"Yeah, I used to watch that when I was a kid," Betty smiled, fluttering her eyelashes and moving closer.

Sarah Johnson walked up, stomping her boots to get Betty's attention. She draped her arm around Xander's neck, "Hi, ya, Betty. What're you doing?"

"Um, just talking about Xander's big white dog and weird housecat."

"They're unique animals. Maybe Geoffrey is under a special Murdoc spell that allows him to look like a Great Dane when his normal appearance is much more frightening!" Sarah said through tight jaws.

Betty let out a nervous giggle, "Surely, you're trolling me, Sarah."

"Just wait 'till Halloween. Geoff's glamour will fade away so you will see his true self," Sarah said.
Nickoli, Sarah's Anansi poked his head out from under her red and black striped hair.

"No way! There's no such thing as glamour. You're talking about magic . . ."

"Magic – Murdoc Magic," Sarah said raising an eyebrow. "Nickoli, my pet spider and I will remove it. Just wait. In three weeks, you will see."

True self? Lynx replayed the phrase in his mind. *Demon . . . only demons hide their true self or physical body. Who am I kidding? I'm no demon – but what am I? I forgot . . .*

In the background, Lynx heard Sarah remind the teen gal that Xander was her boyfriend and to leave them alone. She also heard Sarah promise to reveal Lynx's true form to the girl they called Betty.

No, no, no . . .never again! I will never ever be that ugly creature again! He's a Runt, missing part of an ear and the tail is crooked because . . . because . . ouch! Missing clumps of fur . . . how did that happen? Hot! Help! Nooo! Not me! Not demon – young! Stop! Recognize me! Nooo! Help!

The bear viewed Lynx being swallowed in imaginary flames and smiled to himself. "Good, good. My incantations are working. Soon, that werecat will suffer for allowing humans to influence him." The bear rubbed his paws together.

Chapter 2

Lynx scanned the sky looking for Geoffrey at the same time he focused his other senses on finding a deer or two for themselves for breakfast. Spotting the white griffin high up in the clouds, he smiled to himself, then spied the herd not far ahead. Breaking into a run, hoping the deer didn't hear him, he caught up to them, dropping to a crouch to creep forward, doing his best not to break any twigs or go through dry leaves. With the floor of the forest covered with dry branches, shed leaves and other underbrush, it was hard to avoid it. Lynx kept creeping until he was close enough to the target, a large doe, when he stepped on a large branch. The snap alerted the large buck of the herd to leave where he was grazing to come back to see what was stalking them. He let out a loud bellow to warn of the danger and the does ran away. Lynx sprang up for the chase, jumping over the fallen logs and dashing around rocks, spying two elderly does who slowed down and turned to the left. The werecat turned with them, briefly scanning the sky to make sure Geoffrey was following him. Satisfied that the griffin was going into a dive towards the two deer, he got ready to spring onto the rump of the closest one. when a massive paw slapped him away in midair, sending Lynx into a side spin that Milo would envy. He landed hard on his side.

When he looked up, there was a monster towering over him, with a long snout and massive paws with sharp claws, and long, sharp canine teeth standing on his hind legs.

"Who are you to hunt in my forest?" the bear roared.

"Who are you to say we can't hunt in your forest?" Lynx fired back. Slowly rolling on to his side.

"I do! I'm Artaois! The god of this forest realm! You dare to refuse to answer to me!" The bear god stood on his hind paws, clawing the air with his front paws and bared his teeth.

"I'm Lynx, werecat of the World of Nampa, friend of the Indigo Travelers," Lynx puffed out his chest, trying to ignore the pain in his side from being smacked out of the air.

Geoffrey landed next to Lynx and nudged him with his beak. Lynx moaned, squeezing his eyes shut, he felt himself overcome with dizziness, but forced himself to stay alert. He managed to speak to his friend.

"That hurts, Geoff. Stop."

Geoffrey turned to the bear, "Why did you knock my friend out of the air?"

The bear narrowed his eyes and began to sniff the air. He got a quizzical look in his eyes as he slowly approached the griffin.

"What are you?" the bear snarled, curling his upper lip.

"What do you mean what am I?" Geoffrey responded.

"I mean, you shift from an eagle, to a lion to a larger than normal dog and then settle on a hybrid eagle and lion mix. It's odd because lions don't live in this part of the world. And why would you be friends with this creature that doesn't belong in this world either?"

"I'm a griffin from the World of Curá and have chosen to live in this world with some friends of ours. Lynx, here, is from that same world."

The bear shook his massive head snarling, "Wrong! This werecat is not from that world! You both smell of humans. A most unpleasant scent and you, werecat, should know better. You have memories you have buried long ago that conceal the truth! Humans aren't your friends! You refuse to accept your original shape or what the humans did to you while you were a cub!"

Lynx's jaw dropped when the bear's words struck him. All words flew from his mind and his memories blocked. Closing his mouth, he struggled to roll over to his belly and slowly rise to his feet but couldn't, letting out a whimper and moan, he settled back half on his belly and half on his side.

"Careful, Lynx," Geoff whispered to him.

"What do you say for yourself? Werecat?" Artaois, the self-appointed god of the forest roared.

Staring at the ground, Lynx's stomach grumbled. "I say I'm hungry. You interrupted our hunt for our breakfast. I say you don't have authority to tell Geoffrey and me where or what we can hunt for food. We don't eat more than our share and we take only the infirm, leaving the strong and the young." He shut his eyes from the brightness of the sun, filtering through the trees.

Geoffrey, nodding in agreement, turned to face the bear. "We don't recognize your authority or godship over this forest or over us. We only recognize Albagoth, the Creator of All Worlds!"

Artaois roared, lunging at the griffin, "There is no such thing as a Creator of all Worlds! There is only me! Bear god of all animals! Even you!"

"No, not true. You're the first bear I've ever seen," Geoffrey replied. "There's no bears where I'm from. And since Lynx is from my world, then you're the first bear he's seen."

Lynx lowered his head, flashing on when he was a cub and his spirit wandered to that family of creatures that looked like this bear standing in front of him. Geoff's words struck a false chord with him, but he couldn't bring himself to speak up because he was wavering in and out of consciousness. Suddenly, his mind shifted to a darkness, imprisoned under a burning wooden cage. Burning . . . smoking, heat, creeping towards him and he couldn't move. All he could do was cry out, whimpering. Meowing, hoping to be free.

"Yes, fire, Lynx. Humans did that to you. Werecats shift. Werecats are ugly creatures. Yet you are beautiful and proud. Denying what you know in your heart you really are," sneered Artaois.

"How do you know? There are no other werecats in the World of Nampa. If you've known other werecats, then this is not your original world, either," Lynx said, narrowing his eyes.

Artaois flinched. Lowering himself to all four feet, he wagged his head, shaking slowly as if to chase away flies, he took a deep breath and let it out slowly then spoke, "I don't know. It's just some distant memory or something . . ."

The bear turned away from the other two and lumbered off.

Geoffrey and Lynx stared at the bear's buttocks as he left.

"Can you get up?" Geoff asked, prodding him.

Lynx tried again, but his side and head screamed at him.

"Are you hurt?" Geoff asked.

"Not sure. It might just be my pride. You know what Xander said to me the other day? The pride goes before the fall. I think I had to fall first for my pride to leave," Lynx laughed.

The griffin shook his head, "Well, if you can crack jokes, you're going to be alright. C'mon, get up and let's look at you."

Lynx agreed. Once more he struggled to stand, taking a deep breath and managing to get on all fours, he turned to look at his left side, "It looks like I have a small scratch or bruise from landing against that boulder. But I think I will be okay."

"Walk out a bit so I can see," Geoffrey said. Lynx did as directed. "Yep, there's a small wound, but it isn't bleeding that bad."

"We can finish the hunt. I will get the deer, unless you'd rather have fish," Geoffrey suggested, they began to walk towards a small lake not far from where they were.

"Fish might be better than deer. We always eat deer. Let's take the catch home so Erin can cook it for us. My head hurts and that bear shook me up quite a bit."

An otter pup poked his head out, stood up on his back legs, and sniffed the air. He turned to watch the two off-worlders strolling towards the river.

Chapter 3

Mist rose from the ground and swirled around the yard, giving Lynx an eerie feeling that something wasn't right. Other mists and scents that only Lynx could smell drifted in from the distant mountains. Those scents mixed with another from downtown Nampa that other animals and people would smell.

His ears rose, tuning in to frequencies most humans couldn't hear. In the far distance, he heard soulful sobbing from some person or animal that sounded like the person lost their only friend. Yet he couldn't recognize the voice or make out what the person or creature was saying between sobs. A vision of a kitten huddled under a blanket somewhere pulled his heart strings. Yet he couldn't find it. It was too far away.

"Help me! Not demon cat! Just young werecat cub. Help me!" The small voice whimpered. Lynx shut it somewhere deep inside his mind, refusing to acknowledge it. It wasn't real. It was too scary. Too much pain. Heartache. Not all humans are bad. Can't say it. "It's not me, I can't help you," he muttered to the vision and the cry for help.

Clarence, the white and orange tabby cat that also lived in the Veh house, noticed the werecat's odd behavior. He strode over to Lynx.

"What is it?" Clarence asked. Lynx jumped ten feet high, turned in mid-air and landed in front of the cat. Clarence smiled smugly, enjoying frightening the werecat that always put on a brave, proud and larger than life persona.

"I hear someone or something crying from the depths of his soul," Lynx said. *Did I just say that out loud? If*

Clarence knows I'm hearing something that might not be real, he would tease me to no end. Lynx swallowed hard.

"Nothing, Clarence. Nothing is wrong," Lynx finally said louder, hoping Clarence didn't hear what he said. Lynx mentally crawled back into his reflection. *This world is still foreign to me. I've only been in Nampa for two years. I wanted to live here. I needed to explore other places outside of Curá. Away from my protective home. A place where I can pretend to be something I'm not to those strangers that came to the Veh house. But those who knew me most – well, no one knows me at all.* Lynx quivered inside his skin. *I can't allow anyone to know the real werecat I am. I need this phony persona. I can't allow anyone to see my true form. They'd run in fear of me. Or burn me at the stake. Though, it was tried once before. Over a year ago before Xander and the gang went back to Curá to venture into the Shadowlands.*

Looking out, he saw spirals moving toward him, swirling, almost as if there was a hand reaching through them to grab and shake him. He could feel the hand grabbing him and missing him yet keep trying to. Lynx could sense part of himself trying to avoid it, but it followed him – chasing him.

"This mist is spooky," Lynx said finally. "I see images of spirits and hear voices without bodies." Taking a deep breath and whiff of the air, "And it stinks!"

"All Hallow's Eve is drawing close," Clarence said. "It's the sugar beet factory that is working overtime. I don't smell anything else."

"No, there is something else in the smell, but I can't pinpoint it," Lynx said. Then thought and said, "All Hallow's Eve? What's that?" Lynx sat down, tried to smooth his fur down with a wet paw.

"It's the time of year that spirits walk at night, calling to others, and witches gather in the woods to celebrate their magic, drawing forth the goodness of what they have brought into this year. Humans see the witches as evil and working with the devil." Clarence shrugged. "My staff says the witches aren't evil, but only want to help each other and the world by restoring balance."

"Balance in what?" Lynx asked, glancing around him at the call of a crow cawing above them.

"Balance in nature and in all things. They want to restore the idea that what each person sends out they will get back three-fold." Clarence chuckled as he noticed Lynx was cowering from the various night birds calling and answering each other.

"What has you so jumpy?" the tabby cat finally asked.

"Ever since watching the kids from Xander's school's bonfire two nights ago, every shadow and noise frightens me. Like I need to remember something that is very dangerous to me. Also, I keep expecting a Crow Judge to come and arrest me for violating some law of Curá that I hadn't heard of." Lynx lowered himself further to the ground. "Then I remember the Crow Judges don't monitor the World of Nampa."

"You aren't as tough as you want others to think you are, werecat," Clarence chided. "Relax. You're too hard on yourself." The tabby stood up, stretching his front legs and then his back legs and started heading for the back porch doggy door. "I'm going into a warm bed beside Xander."

"You're going to leave me out here to the witches and ghouls?" Lynx cried.

"Yep. Sure am. My doghouse is warm. My staff put a warm blanket or two in there this morning, so you can crawl under them."

"Night," Lynx muttered, glancing around.

Looking up at the round bright orange moon with a white halo around it, Lynx wondered what truly was out there. The moon called him, but he couldn't make out exactly what it was saying. It appeared larger than normal. Taking a deep breath and letting it out slowly, he stood and walked to the doghouse and went inside. He picked up a blanket, spread it on the ground for padding and picked up another one, laid it on the first one, and put a third blanket over him for extra warmth. He made a mental note to ask Erin for a cushion bed like they got for Geoffrey for inside the house.

Raising his front paws to his face, he spread his toes out, examining them one by one, meditating on how he could use them to improve his deep fear. Or find who was hurting so bad.

"Albagoth, I'm not sure you answer creatures like me. I feel so alone and isolated. I -I-I . . ." Lynx paused in mid-sentence. "I don't know what to say."

Clicking his first toe and his thumb together, just to make sure they still worked, he wished to see who was crying and so deeply hurting. He didn't transport anywhere, though. He stayed right where he was. Frustrated, he yawned, turned over on his side. Then decided to curl up like the big kitten he was shaped to be.

Mists swirled around him, rising and falling, shaped like humans with wings climbing an invisible ladder while others taunted him. Lynx walked alone in the forest, but he couldn't make out where the trees were and where the body of water was.

"You're lost, Lynx. You're not you who you think you are. Can you even see yourself on a clear day?" One of the beings taunted.

"You're such an ugly creature, you are a horrible werecat. You know you're ugly, that's why you hide in the shape of a socially acceptable Maine Coon. You're afraid of seeing your true form." Another said.

"Go away! I know who I am! I am who I want to be!" Lynx barked.

"Ooh! A cat who barks, commands us to go away. What do you say, gentlemen and gentleladies, should we listen to him? I bet he can't even listen to himself!"

"Yeah!" the chorus agreed. They laughed.

"I thought you were angels! You look more like demons to me!" Lynx said snidely.

"Demons?" another stated.

"Angels?" another asked. They laughed with the group.

They cried out, "We are neither what you nor the humans have created. We are just the ones who poke at those who live in fear. You, Lynx Werecat, are afraid of being yourself!"

A loud, mournful cry pierced the jabs and laughter. Lynx growled and hissed at these horrible creatures, and they finally disappeared. He followed the cry up a long and winding path, which led up a steep hill. As he neared the top, the mist cleared. The light from the moon shined on one solitary figure curled in a heap of blankets, sobbing and whimpering, "Help me! It hurts! I didn't do anything. Help me, please."

Lynx carefully walked up to the animal, lifted a paw and gently touched it's back.

"What's wrong, friend?" he asked.

The animal stopped sobbing, looked and burst into flames. Lynx jumped back, screamed.

Lynx managed to fall into a restless sleep, but images of the fire and memories of the bonfire the weekend before haunted him. Not to mention that bear that called himself a god batting him down as if he was a pesky fly from a perfectly good pounce on the rump of a juicy deer. The voices of the teens in the backyard woke him, though. Stretching, he left the warm doghouse to see why they were up so early.

A large pile of flat stones was on the side of the spot where Erin, Xander's mom, usually had her garden. Some of the stones had markings on them and some didn't. Clarence sniffed each stone and the dirt in the garden that Xander and Milo were beginning to flatten out with shovels and then noticed Sarah was coming along, marking where to put each stone with a yellow plastic stake.

"What's going on?" Lynx asked.

"We're laying down stones for a walking meditation path," Xander said.

Lynx yawned, smacked his lips. One of his ears flopped over on its side as if it was too tired to stand up on its own. He struggled to keep his eyes open. Hearing a low muttering, which caught him off guard, he shook his head and started scanning the area to see what the teens were doing.

Sarah and Nickoli, her Anansi guide and companion who looked like a spider were muttering prayers as they laid down each individual stone. *How did the ground get flat so quickly?* he wondered.

Xander, using his ability to read Lynx's mind, turned, "Milo used his wish gift to speed up the process. Now Sarah and Nickoli are blessing each stone. We hope to have this up by tomorrow."

"What's the hurry?" Lynx said. Geoffrey came up next to them.

"Yeah, what's the hurry?" he agreed. Then he asked, "That new kid, Ian Temple, is here. Should I tell Erin to send him back here? Or do you all want to keep this a secret?"

"He knows about Nickoli, if that is what you mean," Sarah said. "We're working with him. And he knows you're a griffin disguised as a Great Dane. So, bring him back."

Xander went up to Lynx, "What happened to your ear?"

"What do you mean?"

"Part of your right ear is missing," he said, reaching out to touch it, "It looks like something bit it off." Lynx looked him in the eyes, taken aback.

"No, I guess I'm wrong. Both ears are whole," Xander blinked and shook his head.

"I think the sun is getting to you," Geoffrey muttered.

"Not sure," Xander rubbed his eyes. A smaller teen, about thirteen or fourteen came in to join the group, with his hands in his pockets, staring at the ground as he shuffled along. He glanced up and forced a smile at everyone.

"What's going on?" Ian asked. Sarah, Xander and Milo explained.

"What's the hurry to get it done?" Lynx asked.

"It's for a presentation we're doing in art class," Sarah said, winking at the others.

"No, it's so we will have a walking meditation path to assist us when we need to focus on staying present," Milo said. "We want to be done by Sunday because it just is a good day to have it finished by."

Lynx watched the group working and his skin started to crawl. The mid-October morning buzzed with energy that he couldn't place. And something wasn't right about the words Sarah was chanting. He wondered if she knew what she was saying. Shaking his head, he got up and walked away.

"What's wrong?" Clarence came up to him. Geoffrey wasn't far behind.

"She is enchanting the path, so it will have a portal. Maybe each step will be a portal. They're asking for trouble." Lynx's voice trembled.

"How do you know that?" Clarence asked, not sure what to think.

"I don't know, but I just know they aren't sure what they're doing. Also, that Ian kid is very unhappy. He may try to use it without them knowing."

"No, he wouldn't dare . . ." Clarence said. "He can't get into our backyard without us knowing it."

"I agree with Lynx," Geoffrey said. "We better warn them."

"What if they know what it will do and Albagoth will be guiding the portals?" Clarence suggested.

Lynx and Geoffrey stared at him, shocked he would suggest that.

"What do you know about Albagoth?" They demanded.

The domestic long-hair shrugged his shoulders, "Nothing. I just heard Sarah and Nickoli utter that name as they chanted with each stone placement. I think it's a blessing or something."

Lynx set his jaw, wagging his head back and forth and stalked over to them. The end of his tail jerked with anger. Stopping at Sarah's side, he said, "Quit! I don't like this! You don't know what you're doing!"

Sarah paused to look at him, surprised, almost dropping the sage and sweetgrass stick she was using to bless the stones the boys placed.

"What do you mean I don't know what I'm doing?" She fumed.

"You're making each stone a possible portal to some place. It's dangerous!"

Sarah laughed. She glanced at Nickoli, who rolled two of his eight eyes and waved a right foot as if pushing away the werecat's concerns.

"We're Murdocs, Lynx. We know what we're doing. Sage Tomás went through how to build this and what to say as we built it the last time we met with him.

There won't be any portals," Nickoli smiled, showing his long, jagged fangs.

"Besides, if there will be, it will be the center one," Sarah quipped, putting her long black and red hair behind her ear to get it out of her eyes.

Lynx narrowed his golden eyes and looked serious. "I still don't like it! What if you all use this while Geoffrey and I are out hunting for our breakfast or dinner and you are transported to another world? We won't be able to follow you or protect you!"

"Fair question, Lynx. We won't know for sure. What if we say none of us will use it until you all are present to go with us?" Xander said.

"No!" Lynx said, his thoughts spinning, not able to focus. Lowering his head, began to feel woozy, smelling other scents that weren't in the bundle Sarah had but he couldn't place them. "I still don't like this!"

"It's fine to object, but we aren't going to unmake it," Milo said. "We need this path to assist us with learning from Sage Tomás and Albagoth. Sage Tomás assured us it wouldn't take anyone anywhere except into a deep, meditative state. But the next time I journal, I will ask that question and share the answer with you."

Lynx nodded, inhaling a putrid smell of burning leaves and other odors he couldn't place, which caused his head to spin and his legs to weaken. Lynx slowly staggered away. Xander cocked his head to one side and followed his friend. As Lynx walked away, he heard Ian asking what it was like to go through a portal and visit other worlds. Xander heard the question, too, so he stopped and turned back.

Lynx heard Sarah and Milo tell Ian not to use the path without them. In Lynx's mind, he saw the younger teen smiling to himself; he was aware Ian was planning something. He wanted to warn Ian not to follow through, but he couldn't. Something was pulling him away. Some force was messing with his senses, pulling his soul back to another time. Slowly, he raised his head to the early afternoon sun; it was glowing, moving in fast circles and appearing to grow and then reduce with strange waves going in front of it. He couldn't help but think that is was odd for it to do. Then everything appeared to go black.

A fire burned off in a meadow, Lynx saw himself heading up the hill, because he heard an animal crying from it. He heard laughter, some boys not native to the World of Nampa, were running away, chanting, "Die demon cat! Die demon cat! We finally got you. Die! Your punishment awaits down below with the other demon cats!"

"No, demon cats don't have souls!" Another said. "But die it will. Serves it right for coming into our village looking for handouts!"

"What's wrong, Lynx? Clarence mentioned you were having nightmares and not sleeping right." Xander asked.

"Not demon cat," Lynx muttered. "Not demon cat! Hot! Hurts! Help me! Help me." Lynx muttered, his eyes rolling up in his skull. "Souls. Werecats have souls. Help."

Chapter 4

Swirling and moving as if swimming through the air, mists vied with each other to see which individual thread could make the thinnest line and who could make the most elaborate design to gain the master's attention to be called on for the next assignment. Strong smells of fireweed, feline locoflower, cheat grass and worm wood rose from a large black cauldron.

"Enough!" a stern voice barked in the corner of the cave. The mists all ran for the iron cauldron over the fire. "You all are annoying me! I can't concentrate on what this werecat is thinking or planning or how my incantations are working." A massive, grizzly bear walked out holding more feline locoflower in his paw. "You're driving him mad, Master," said a small mouse, washing his paws, smiling, showing a few broken teeth, giggling with delight.

"That is my plan! But there are others that are getting in the way, preventing him from fleeing his new home. We can't allow him to get too comfortable with the humans," the bear replied as he walked over to the cauldron bubbling over a roaring fire, crushed up the dried dark yellow and black petals while forming the incantation in his mind. The bear took a hold of the large paddle inside it and started stirring the contents, while chanting an incantation out loud that would be sent out for Lynx to smell and influence his mind and body to show him a healthy fear of humans. A fox stood on a large boulder watching and listening.

"Artaois, Lynx was raised by a human on Curá. He's comfortable with them," the fox said.

"How do you know? The first I heard of that place was from that hybrid animal that calls itself a griffin!"

The fox wavered, his thoughts spinning. "I just know. I get flashes of scenes and humans when I observe him and his friend." The fox pawed the ground, trying calm his quaking legs. "I heard them say they recognize a creator of all worlds."

"There is only one world, Fox! This one! I'm the god of it! It's up to me to monitor the wild animals and the magical ones, like Lynx. He's out of his element. He needs to remember how the humans treated him eons ago."

"Was it really eons ago?" asked a small fox cub that was listening at his big brother's feet.

Artaois roared. "Of course not, you fool!" Artaois paused considering his words—trying to remember something but there was a large brick wall preventing him from retrieving it. All he could glimpse was a snip-it of a werecub and himself as a cub running away from two humans. The werecub was on fire. Closing his eyes tight, he shook his head. What he just saw wasn't this world at all.

"I can't smell anything, Lord Artaois. What're you cooking?" said a mouse. The question brought the bear god back to the present.

"It isn't for you, you fool! It's a spell to influence that horrible demon werecat!" Artaois snarled.

An otter pup, listening quietly in a pile of underbrush ventured forward and spoke up, "Artaois, I've seen Lynx and that griffin he's friends with. They love their humans and the humans who care for them love them, too. You're taking an unfortunate incident from Lynx' past and saying it will happen again. You don't know that it will. Let Lynx stay where he is. Stop tormenting him like this."

Artaois turned abruptly to face the otter, raising his strong, powerful arms, baring his sharp, teeth and roared. All the smaller creatures ran away, except the otter pup, who looked the massive bear in his deep, brown eyes.

"You don't tell me what to do! I'm the god of this forest. I tell these creatures what to do and what to be afraid of and I will remind Lynx that his werecat family once worshipped me, prayed to me and gave me offerings to protect them, guide them and fulfill all their needs. All creatures of this forest fear me! Lynx has strayed from that faith. I intend to bring him back. All the creatures in this forest and the forests across this world fear me."

"I'm not afraid of you, Artaois. I provide for myself," said the brave, young otter.

"You will fear me by the time I get done here! Leave my sight! Only those who fear me are allowed in my presence!" the bear god turned back to the kettle and started stirring the contents again.

"Besides, how do you know the werecat's family once worshipped you? I heard you admit that you don't know how you know any this," the otter confronted him.

"How dare you use my words against me!" Artaois snarled, turning with a large branch he was stirring the pot with and shook it at the otter cub. "Leave my sight!"

The pup stood on his back legs, washing his whiskers, but not moving his eyes away from the bear. The bear growled. "I command you to leave my sight or you will end up on this magic potion!"

The pup smiled, giggling. "Wanna try?" his eyes twinkled. The bear god made an abrupt move toward the otter pup, who turned and ran away, laughing, loving to taunt the stupid self-absorbed bear.

"If you're such a powerful god, Artaois, why do you need to brew a spell for Lynx?" the otter pup yelled from a safe distance under a bush.

Artaois roared loudly. "Out of my sight!"

"I am out of your sight. But never out of your mind. My words will haunt you."

Lynx whimpered loudly, sobbed, "Noo! Noo! Stop! Stinging! I'm innocent! Please stop!" He rolled around, patting himself, twisting the blanket around and around his long, fluffy body until he couldn't move. "Let me go! I'm not a demon! Honest! I'm just a kitten! A baby. Have mercy!"

Mercy is for the beautiful and the confident! came a voice. *"You are neither!"*

Lynx observing the dream couldn't pinpoint what the creature sneering and taunting him looked like. But it was clear it wasn't a friend. Lynx saw himself walking away, when the dream self wanted to fight, but was afraid of being overpowered. Weak, unsure – knowing deep down he wouldn't survive and maybe even deserved to be punished for being born. Indeed, why was he born? What is a werecat for? What purpose? Especially one that is so small, ugly and others seemed to hate.

The snapping, popping and stinging continued to threaten the small cub, who wanted to fight, but couldn't. All he could do was whimper. Distant voices spoke as if they were calling down a long funnel way above him; looking up through the orange flames, the dream self let out a deep anxious breath.

"Lynx, Lynx, what's wrong?" Xander and others called to him.

"He's being bewitched," Geoffrey said.

"How'd you know?" Sarah asked.

"Milo, go get Mom," Xander directed. Milo nodded and dashed towards the back door.

Geoffrey prodded the unconscious werecat. "Wake up, buddy. Come back to us."

Lynx stirred, inhaled deeply and slowly exhaled, as his eyelids fluttered, trying to open. It was a struggle, though, because it felt like they were glued shut. Finally, they opened, and the bright early afternoon sun blinded him. Opening more slowly, he glanced at all the concerned faces. Next, he heard pounding of several pairs of feet running out, mixed with the concerned voices of Xander's parents.

Oh, great, that's all I need. More parental figures oohing and awing over me.

"What's going on?" Erin and Mark said together.

"Get out the way, let me get close," Erin urged. The teens moved. "One at a time, what happened?"

"Lynx, can you sit up?" Mark asked.

"I'll try. But please, don't pamper me. I can manage," Lynx said, rolling on his side, then wincing, remembering his tangle with the bear earlier in the morning while he and Geoffrey were out hunting.

"What happened? Your side has a large wound on it!" Erin said. "Why didn't you tell me? I could've treated that this morning. Instead, you and Geoffrey bring me fish to clean and cook for you two."

"That's my staff!" Clarence said, thrusting out his chest. Ian, Erin and Mark heard him say, "Meowup," smiling smugly.

"Clarence, stop boasting. Mom, Lynx was telling us to be careful of how we blessed the walking path, then he started slurring his words and staggering as if he was drunk or drugged," Xander said in a rush.

"And he mentioned something about the air smelling funny," Milo added.

"If you ask me, I say that bear is messing with Lynx's head and mind," Geoffrey spat out.

"What bear?" everyone asked, looking at him.

"That bear that knocked Lynx away from a potential kill this morning. That's where he got that wound on his side. Lynx and I thought it wouldn't be that bad. Maybe just a bruise. There wasn't any blood," Geoffrey.

"Bears can't brew spells," Mark, Xander's father dismissed. "They're smart and intimidating, but they ain't witches or warlocks. If you two tangled with a bear it was because you two encroached on his territory. You better learn how to distinguish what animals' scents are and what they mean. Since you are still new here, hunting rules are different. If you all can't learn that, then let me and Erin provide for you."

Lynx and Geoffrey both made sour faces. "I'm not eating dog food, Mark," Geoffrey said.

A squirrel dropped off the telephone wire to the top of the redwood fence and scurried along the top.

"I'm not eating dry kitty kibble either," Lynx said. "Just give me my own bottle of milk and I will open it myself." Glancing at the squirrel, "Or eat that squirrel over there."

Mark's jaw dropped.

"Besides, the area we were hunting in wasn't that bear's territory." Geoffrey countered.

"How do you know?" Mark fired back.

"I just know. Call it my animal instinct. That bear called himself a god and said those deer were off limits to Lynx and me."

"Yeah. I want to know who elected him god and where was he when Geoff and I took down all those deer last year?" Lynx added.

The squirrel paused to admonish Lynx for that threat.

All the humans joined in with the squirrel. Lynx rolled his eyes. Rolling on to his belly, Lynx said, "Okay, they're too small. Anyway, please give me some space. I doubt that bear can do me any harm since he lives up in the forest and doesn't know how to get to our subdivision."

Erin inserted two fingers in her mouth, took a deep breath and blew it between them, shutting everyone up to look at her.

"Now that I have your attention. Lynx, you will not be eating any squirrels. We can make sure you and Geoffrey have fresh meat of any kind you two desire. And bear gods are unknown in this world except in mythology." She paused, blushing as she considered the albino griffin.

"What do you mean, Mom?" Xander asked. "I never heard of bear gods or read about them in any lore books. Milo, Sarah and I have scoured thousands of books on mythology since we first met Geoffrey and Lynx."

Erin smiled devilishly, "I finally know something you three don't . . ." she giggled. "There is a little-known mythology, I don't remember what country it is from, that talked about a bear god called Artaois . . ."

"That was that bear's name," Lynx and Geoffrey stated.

Later that night, Geoffrey and Lynx talked about it. "I still want to hunt for our food. Maybe not every day, but I like being out in the woods," Lynx said.

"So, do I. It reminds me of back home and allows me to relax more in the fresh air."

"Should we worry about that bear?" Lynx wondered. Geoffrey shrugged.

"Not sure, but we should tell Erin before we go hunting so she won't prepare food for us."

"Yes, we should." Lynx yawned. He took a deep breath and then let it out slowly. He twisted around to see the herbs and bandages that Erin patched him up with. He licked and bit at them. "I wish I could remove those. It hurts."

"It will feel better. Let's try to sleep," Geoffrey said, trying to suppress a yawn.

"Night," Lynx yawned again, stood up and started walking to the doghouse.

"Night," Geoffrey said, standing and walking towards the house.

Lynx turned to watch the griffin squeeze himself through the dog door. In order to do that, he had to get down on his belly and crawl through, like what a Great Dane would do. Lynx chuckled, *that glamour sure fits him.*

Chapter 5

Lynx burrowed under the warm blankets, sighed and fell into a restless sleep. The air still had a strange scent of herbs and flowers he wasn't familiar with. Images of that bear god floated through his mind. Lynx couldn't understand why the bear wanted him to be afraid of humans. There had to be something more to it. Taking a deep breath, he let it out fast. *Albagoth, please let me know what is bothering me. Show me what this bear god wants of me and why he hates me so much.*

Gradually, he fell into a restless sleep. Fleeting dream images of a werecub walking through a village, scared, alone and not sure of itself. A woman with a broom swept the cub off the wooden walking path. As it continued to roam the village, hoping to find food, he heard some kids.

"Look, it's a demon werecat! Let's get it!" the boys shouted, chasing after it. They managed to grab it. But the werecub, being small and scrawny managed to escape them. Spotting a wagon that was turned over off the beaten path, he decided to crawl under it to hide. The boys laughed, all in good fun.

"We got you, demon cat! You all are scum. We burn you like the demon you are. Since we know demons love fire and nothing will hurt you," The boys chanted. The werecub couldn't see their faces. He heard the fire start, and the flames grew fast, snapping, crackling. Soon, the flames were threatening him. The cub turned around, tried to dig a hole to get out, but he was weak from hunger.

"Die, demon cat! Die!" The dream images shifted to a meadow. A bear pranced around a kettle, chanting, "Remember true shape. Remember humans are evil. Wild creatures stay away. Burn. Those who don't burn become Demon once more. Little werecub. Demons burn."

Lynx whimpered loudly, sobbed, "Noo! Noo! Stop! Stinging! I'm innocent! Please stop!" he rolled around, patting himself, twisting the blanket around and around his long, fluffy body until he couldn't move. "Let me go! I'm not a demon! Honest! I'm just a kitten! A baby. Have mercy!"

Mercy is for the beautiful and the confident! came the dream image.

"Lynx! Lynx, wake up!" Geoffrey, the albino Griffin stuck his head in the doghouse. "You're having a nightmare. You're going to wake up the household."

Geoff gently touched the werecat on the shoulder. Lynx woke up, eyes wide and claws out.

"What?!" He spotted the griffin and relaxed. "Oh, Geoffrey. I'm glad it's you."

"I can hear your heart racing a mile a minute. Sit up and relax. When you're ready, want to come hunt with me? We can talk about your dream."

Lynx sat up, looked down at his stomach. "I'm not sure I want to talk about it. You'll think I'm a wimp."

Geoffrey chuckled, "You're no wimp, Lynx. We all have our weaknesses. I think this world is enough different than the one we came from, that it brings up new fears we both haven't dealt with since we were young. I am there to listen to you when you are ready to discuss what is going on with you, though."

Lynx smiled. "Yeah, I know. Give me a minute. A good hunt might be what I need."

"You have it," the griffin nodded and backed out of the doghouse.

Lynx sat up, looked at his front paws, images of his dreams and the charred face he saw frightened him to no end. He shuddered, lowering himself back to the ground and tried to bury himself under the blankets.

A loud thud shook the large doghouse, startling the werecat. Next came claws slowly scraping along the tile roof. Lynx didn't want to look up or get out even though his stomach growled and rumbled.

"Boo!" Clarence hung his head over the opening.

"EEYeow!" Lynx jumped out from under the covers. Clarence laughed.

"Clarence, what do you think you're doing scaring me like that?"

"You've been a scaredy cat for the last two days, Lynx. I'm not sure what's going on with you. You're normally so brave and sure of yourself. Now I think it is all a big phony persona, so others will think you're hot stuff when you are a weakling," Clarence turned his ears so he could hear the werecat better.

"I'm no weakling!" Lynx sat up, jutted out his chest and lifted his chin up.

"Then prove it!" Clarence taunted.

"How?" Lynx demanded.

"I don't know. I'll think of something. When I do, I will let you know. Anyway, my staff wants to know if you're hungry. She has food ready for us."

Lynx wrinkled up his lips and lifted his chin up in the air, "Is it that god-awful canned stuff that passes for cat food?" he spat.

"Yep. It's good." Clarence licked his lips.

"No, it isn't! It's cooked and tastes like – like- I don't know what you all call it here in this world—like feces!"

"Lynx! That's not nice to say. I don't insult your food. Besides, Erin tries very hard to buy the food she thinks we'll like," Clarence hopped down off the roof and approached him.

Lynx frowned. The back door opened and closed. Both cats heard someone coming out. Lynx took a deep breath and let it out, lowering his head.

"I'm used to fresh meat. Besides, Geoffrey and I will probably go hunting in a little bit." He looked at his cat companion. "I didn't mean to insult you. I know Erin tries. She and I have had many late-night talks after everyone goes to bed. Did you know there are nights she can't sleep because she's worried about the boys?" Lynx asked.

"Yes, I know. Those are the times I do my best to get her to go back to bed. I've tried to sooth her but can't always show her my ability to use her language like I can with Xander and Milo."

Lynx cocked his head to one side, "That day is coming when she will accept your ability to talk, my friend. Come, let's go see who came outside."

"Lynx! Clarence! It's time to come in!" Xander called.

"What do you want?" Lynx puffed out his chest, putting on his tough façade.

"Knock it off! I hope you slept better than you have been doing. Come on, Mom made something special for you, Lynx. It isn't canned cat food," Xander gave a weak smile. "That argument you all had with her yesterday got her thinking. She fixed the fish you and Geoffrey brought home yesterday morning.

"We'll see about that!" Lynx held his tail and head high as he headed for the animal door. Clarence, much lighter on his feet due to being smaller and thinner, raced ahead of the werecat, who was too busy being haughty and stuck up.

Xander just wagged his head, chuckling.

"I hope your side feels better. Anyway, come in and see what Mom prepared for you," Xander reached out a hand to stroke the fluffy werecat, who leaned into his hand and began to purr unconsciously. Then noticed the smile on his human friend's face and realized he was making a humming sound. "You're just a big kitten with a soft heart, Lynx. You aren't tough at all."

"Just don't let the griffin know I purred," Lynx whispered.

"Your secret is safe with me," Xander made a zipping motion on his lips, then smiled.

They walked into the house. Lynx, smelling the baked fish from the family room, turned to see Geoffrey standing in the utility area, which was between the family room and the kitchen. He didn't look happy.

"What's wrong?" Lynx asked him. The griffin shrugged.

"Let's go for a walk in the woods. Clarence said you're still having nightmares and I sense something wrong in the air. You mentioned it yesterday afternoon before you fainted."

"Okay. But first, I want some food," Lynx said, pushing by the large griffin that took up most of the entryway.

Erin, small, with shoulder length dark hair, greeted the werecat as she put down a large bowl of fresh baked salmon mixed with fresh vegetables and herbs from her garden. Taking a deep breath, to savor the scent, he grinned.

"Thank you, Erin. It smells delicious." He lowered his head and began devouring every morsel. Finally, he stopped to take a deep breath, and let it out. "It was wonderful. You have to teach me how to cook."

"I would think with your thumbs, you could provide enough food for yourself, Lynx," Erin replied, smiling.

The werecat turned to see Geoffrey waiting, "Did you eat, Geoff?"

The griffin nodded, narrowing his eyes. "Let's go. Something is bugging me and I'm not sure what it is."

They went toward the back door, Lynx paused, stretched up a paw, grasped the doorknob with his flexible toes and turned it, "Yep, I figured I could open it like Xander and the others," he said smugly.

They raced outside onto the covered porch into the yard, the griffin spread his wings and started flapping. Once he was in the yard, Geoffrey jumped up into the air.

"Where do I meet you?" Lynx said.

"In the clearing under that large fir tree we were at the other day," Geoffrey called down.

Lynx nodded, sat on his hunches, raised his paws pads up, and snapped his toes while visualizing the clearing. He vanished from Xander's yard and appeared under the tree. Not far away, there was the lake that they had fished at after they met the bear.

The sun was still rising, but there was a slight chill, being early October by the human's calendar. "Odd that they would measure time like that," Lynx mused.

The air had that strange scent of burning bushes and wood mixed with other odors that the werecat couldn't place. Whatever it was, it gave him an odd sensation that he should be remembering something. Horrors- something- burning, like hair or fur – suddenly the face of an ugly werecat that was twisted in agony came to Lynx's mind. It let out a series of pain filled moans that shook Lynx to his core. Lynx screamed as he backed away from an image that was so real, he had to run.

Something stopped him. "Lynx, what's wrong?" Lynx wasn't stopping. He kept running as fast as he could until he ran into a tree, waking an owl.

"Who who's there?" said the owl. He twisted his head around, looked down, and saw the stunned werecat. "Who, you, Lynx, forgotten your way. Remember the image you refuse to admit to. When you fear something, you need to run to it, not away from it."

"Lynx," Geoffrey cried, catching up to him. "Are you okay?"

Lynx rubbed his head, looked up at the owl and noticed other small animals were gathered around, too. Suddenly, a heat rose from his belly to his face, and he felt foolish. "I think I am." Looking at the owl, "What do you mean I need to remember something I am afraid of? I'm a werecat. I have excellent memory."

"You may think you do, but there is one shape you have suppressed, out of fear of being rejected. You like wearing a pretty body and have an airy personality. Remember and become that true self," Owl replied.

"But . . ." Lynx said. "I'm being bewitched. That bear . . ."

"Artaois? He is nothing. A fallen critter who is from a land he doesn't remember. You're connected to him, but neither understand it. He's envious because you aren't afraid of the two-legged. And he remembers what you forgot, knows you ought to be afraid, too. Healing, my son. Go with your friend."

Lynx thought of the owl's words. He stood up, glanced at Geoffrey. They walked off, but Lynx was blown away, the owl's words replayed in his mind. "Wait a minute. That owl sees me. He sees . . ." he turned and ran back to the tree. Looking up, he found the owl was back asleep. "Hey, hey you. Can I ask one more question?"

The owl opened one eye, "You're disturbing my sleep. But go on."

"Do you see my real self?"

"Yes. I see your true form and it is beautiful. I see your soul, Lynx. Runt of the litter, you had talents that your brothers and sisters didn't. Go, find the runt, he is still inside of you waiting to be loved and accepted. Now, go away and let me sleep. I'm burning daylight."

"How do I find him?" Lynx asked, but the owl was softly snoring.

"C'mon, Lynx, let's go for that walk," Geoffrey called. "I don't know who you're talking to."

"That white owl up in the tree" Lynx pointed. Looking up again, he didn't see it. "It must have flown off or something."

The birds were flying around. Lynx noticed an otter family heading to the water. One little pup kept looking back, not wanting to follow his family. He heard the mom say that the pup wasn't to run off like he usually did. Lynx noticed that the pup was looking at them with concern, like he wanted to tell them something.

"What did you want to say?" Lynx asked, as Geoffrey led them to the water.

"I wanted to discuss those nightmares. My grandsire always said to pay attention to your dreams because they could mean something."

Lynx shook his head, blinked his eyes, scanning the low skies and landscapes, not wanting to think about the dreams. Geoff asked again. Frowning, he said, "I keep seeing myself as a werecub either in a den with my other litter mates or walking in a village I don't remember. Then the scenes switches to a werecub trapped under a burning wagon." Lynx shrugged.

"Didn't you tell us several years ago that Tarrier rescued you from a burning wagon? That he healed your wounds and taught you to shift?" Geoff looked at him.

"Yeah, well . . . that is what he said. I don't remember it very well. All I know was I wasn't a native of Curá and Tarrier never talked much about where he found me. I mean, if I was a native of Curá, there would be other werecats there. I was the only one. And I had to hide my shape. According to that owl, I need to remember my true shape."

"What's wrong with your true shape or body?"

"I rather not say. It's ugly and may have scars. Tarrier said it would scare people."

"So, you became what others would be comfortable with," Geoffrey said.

Lynx sat down by the lake and stared into the ripples caused by the otter family swimming and other animals and fish. Also, there was a slight breeze. He took a deep breath and let it out slowly, considering his friend's words.

"I guess so. Also, I don't think I want to scare anyone. The folks in the village of Kent chased me out with brooms and torches, calling me demon after Tarrier assisted me to get my thumbs. It frightened them to have someone like me who is supposed to be a pet and not be able to provide for myself. I'm not a tame animal, but I like living with humans. For the most part, they have been good to me and I will protect them, too." Lynx looked up. "But that bear seemed to think I should be a wild animal and act like that. What am I to do?"

"Stay away from the bear. You have to live the way that is right for you," Geoff replied.

"Yeah – but the fire – the wagon. It calls me. Like that bon fire the other night we watched. I felt like I belonged to it. I wanted it to consume me and I wanted to consume it. But at the same time, I'm frightened by it." Lynx lowered his head to take a drink of water.

Geoff weighed the words he heard. "I don't know what to tell you. I do think we better be careful. That bear is probably watching us." Geoffrey lowered his head to drink, too.

The otter pup wandered off down the stream to the other side of the lake and managed to find a ride on the back of a deer who was running with its herd towards fresh grass and tender berries before the freeze came.

Over the mountains far from that pleasant lake, Artaois waddled out of his cave, raised his nose in the air to take a deep whiff of the various animal scents floating in the air.

"That werecat and the creature he's friends with are back in my woods," he muttered.

"Want us to go shake up him up, boss?" suggested some snakes.

"Yeah, we can give them the fright of their lives, so they get the message that they don't belong here," said another snake.

Artaois roared. "No! I will take care of it! I'm using the right ingredients to get the message through. I must remind him how dangerous humans are! He must see them for what they are! Two-faced! Remind him . . . he's in danger of being consumed by the fire that scarred him."

"But he has no scars," said the otter pup, sticking his head up from a small puddle near the bear's brew kettle.

"Where did you come from?" the bear scowled.

"I hopped a ride on a deer. Look, I observe that werecat and his friend. They're harmless. He has no scars. Why do you want to hurt him?"

"He's a shapeshifter, pup! He's the only one in this world and he doesn't belong here. He's hiding his true form. He's afraid. Fire- all consuming. He must remember those scars were at the hands of humans!"

The otter pup shook his head, "No, not remember. My aunt says sometimes it's okay not to remember. Need to stay hidden."

"Maybe you can go to where that werecat lives and threaten the human family he lives with. Once he sees them afraid, then he will see how dangerous humans are," a rodent suggested.

"Me? Go into a human village? I wouldn't even know how to get there." Then he thought "Bears that go into the human world get shot."

"Go in at night. You can do it," the fox said. "That owl can help. You must get through to the werecat. He must leave this world. It's too dangerous for him."

"No, this world is peaceful for him. Leave him alone!" said the otter pup.

"Boss, you could consult your crystal ball to see what to do," chimed one of the mischievous coyote pups who often hang out in Wicca ceremonies during rituals.

"Crystal ball? What's that?" Artaois demanded.

"A clear, round glass that gifted seers use to answer questions," answered the coyote. He smiled devilishly. "They aren't usually around these parts, though."

Artaois sneered, "Where would I find one of those?" Then changing his thoughts to the owl. He stroked his chin, sitting up against a large boulder. "Hmm, maybe I could consult the owl. Maybe I could. After all, somehow, I, too, know stuff about that werecat that he doesn't. And I don't know how I know this. Except I am a god that is how I know. I can make things happen. His life will be all mine to destroy."

The little otter trembled, scared of what the bear concluded. Backing up, his mind shifted quickly, wondering what to do. After turning to run down the hill towards the stream, he paused. A quiet voice deep inside of him urged him to be still and listen. The otter pup sat down and turned his eyes inward, *I'm here.*

Protect the werecat, the still quiet voice within directed him. *Urge him to walk the circle path with many lines. I will send another to deal with the bear god.*

The otter pup nodded. *How do I urge the werecat to do that?*

Go to the owl in the tree. He's only seen when one needs him.

Chapter 6

The little otter pup made it back to his nest in the other side of the forest, ignored the call of his aunt and continued to run to the tree where he knew the white owl would be waking up since the sun was setting.

"Mister Owl, Mister Owl, could you assist me?" the little otter pup asked.

The owl opened his large yellow eyes "Who who who's there?"

"Me! Wayohm. I have need to find the werecat. Can you assist me?"

The large white owl twisted his head then peered down at the wiggly otter pup.

"Who sent you?" He blinked with interest.

"The Creative Force that is connecting all of us. The still voice that speaks within me."

The owl nodded, "Go on."

The pup shrugged, "What else do you need?"

"Manx the Snowshoe lynx that walks with ancient of days. The voice within connects with all has a name – genderless – can be anything and anyone. Visions, my son, you have seen them. Even dreams. How come you by the knowledge?"

Wayohm shrugged, "I just know. My grandpap taught me but said not to share it with anyone till they showed they would listen. Few understand. Say animals don't have spirits or souls."

"Not true. If it were true, the misguided bear wouldn't have named himself god of this forest," answered the owl.

"Where can I find the werecat?" Wayohm asked again.

"I will call for help. The eagle will come to take you to the human village where the werecat and his griffin friend live. But be careful. The humans might make a pet of you." The owl fluttered his wings and feathers, closing and opening his eyes drifting off. Aware the pup was still there, added.

"Now, I need to prepare for my evening hunt. Be safe, little Wayohm. Lead Lynx away from the fire that will consume him. Help him find the authentic self he fears."

"I will protect him from the bear, too."

"Brave otter, allow Manx to deal with the bear. Go to the meadow and wait for your lift.

Wayohm nodded to show his understanding and raced to the meadow. In the distance he saw his nest mates and parents watching him. His mom, dad and uncle called to him.

He stopped in the meadow, scanning the sky, watching the lazy clouds drift across the orange and gold setting sun. A dark spot flew across it, then abruptly went into a dive; he then realized what it was. The eagle swooped down and scooped him up. As they flew above the trees and other forest animals, Wayohm watched the deer and other residents watching him. Some pointed and laughed. Others appeared fearful. The little otter dismissed their responses because he knew in his heart, they didn't know his mission.

Gradually, the forest was far behind them. The eagle's talon dug into his skin, but he mentally sent healing vibes to the area. Watching the ground, he noticed the human roadways, with their metal machines rushing to who knew were. The metal machines usually scared him when he got close to a roadway and wanted to cross to get to another river. From this height, they looked more like ants—who were always busy going places and trying to carry more than they were able. Wayohm wondered if the humans ever slept.

With the freeway far behind them, houses were coming into view. He called to the Eagle to help him find the house with the symbol path in the backyard. He imagined it was a smaller circle within a larger one with broken lines and few solid lines leading to the smaller one.

The eagle spotted it before the little otter did, so the eagle slowly descended into the backyard with the path. The otter saw a large doghouse with a white cat laying on top and the albino griffin, who appeared to be glowing in the setting sun. The air started to feel chilly, it being late October by the human calendar. All Hallow's Eve was around the corner.

Once down, Wayohm wondered what to do now. He started to explore the walking path.

"Don't go over there," he heard a gruff voice, startling Wayohm, who jumped straight up and turned in mid-air as he fell back down to face the albino griffin.

"What's your name? Aren't you out of your element here?" Geoffrey said.

"I'm Wayohm. Yep, I am out of my forest. I'm here to warn the werecat that the bear god is out to ruin him. He's in extreme danger." The little otter turned back to the walking path. "What's that? And is it dangerous?"

Geoffrey shrugged. "I don't know. My friends built that for meditation purposes. My sensors tell me that it is a portal to another dimension, and they don't believe me."

"Sensors?" Wayohm turned back to the griffin and approached him.

"My instincts. My Grandsire called them intuition. My human friends don't believe me, though. They haven't walked it yet," Geoff said.

Wayohm stood on his back feet to sniff at the griffin. "What're you doing in this world? If Artaois knew you were here, he'd be targeting you to scare you away."

Geoffrey laughed, shaking his head, "Who is Artaois?"

"He's the bear god who rules all animals of the forest. And you're a wild animal, aren't you?"

Geoffrey threw back his head and laughed. "He can't control me. I don't answer to a pseudo god figure. And, no, I'm not a wild animal. I am a tame, sophisticated griffin."

Wayohm sucked in a large breath and let it out in a harsh hiss. "Don't say that! Artaois hears all things! He's all-knowing!"

"Sorry, if I don't believe in him. He can't hurt me. Besides, I know the Creator of All Worlds is the only one who allows us freedom of belief." Geoffrey replied, turning toward the paw steps behind him. He saw Lynx coming up to them, yawning.

"Who're you talking to, Geoffrey?" Lynx said. "Xander and Milo should be home from school soon."

"Milo had a game tonight, so they stayed. Erin gave them money to eat at the snack bar."

"That's right." Lynx looked down and saw the otter. "River otter. Why aren't you in your river?"

"I've come to warn you to stay away from the forest. Artaois is out to hurt you. He's the bear god. He's very real--flesh and blood. He says you are in danger from the humans and will be hunted down. Also, you're hiding from who you really are," the otter said quickly.

"I've been having nightmares. And seeing this bear," Lynx said slowly. Wayohm noticed a faraway look in the werecat's eyes. "I-I-I," he paused, gathering his thoughts. "I wanted it to just be dreams and memories of the time the boys from my birthplace set me on fire. I can beat it. I'm just experiencing doubts about my new home. No one can scare me away from here. I know Xander's family has accepted me. I'm safe here."

"Maybe you are. I know for a fact the bear god won't stop his attack on you until you leave this world. I've seen him gather the herbs, mix the potions and stir while uttering the spells to influence you. You need to leave here, Mr. Werecat. Your life is at stake."

"Mr. Werecat? That's a new one. I'm Lynx."

The otter turned around to stare at the walking path.

"How did you find me?" Lynx asked, noticing the otter's interest in the path. He approached him.

"The Snowy Owl told me where to find you. The griffin says this is a portal," the otter turned to face Lynx.

"It is if you make it to the center. Sarah, the Murdoc Princess helped the boys design and build it. I heard her and her Anansi muttering a blessing that sounded like they were building a bridge to another world. But I don't think they know what they were doing. None have them tried it yet," Lynx explained.

The otter walked towards it.

"Don't go there," Lynx and Geoffrey cautioned him.

"I have to check this out. Lynx, this is your chance to find what you're looking for. A safe home for yourself where the bear god can't reach you."

"I'm not running from him. Wayohm. I heard you tell Geoff your name," Lynx walked up to him.

The otter turned, "What do you really want? I mean, you might not fear him now. But there has to be something you are afraid of and something you really desire?"

Lynx paused, sitting down, to think. "I will answer that when you come back here and talk with us."

Wayohm turned back to Lynx and Geoffrey.

"I want to find my true self. I've been called a demon one too many times in my life. Tarrier, the one who took me after saving me from under a burning wagon, taught me how to hide my burn scars and true body. He said it would frighten the villagers of Kent and others. He said all werecats are ugly and fierce looking. My scars only made it worse. He taught to me hide it by teaching me to shapeshift. Here in the World of Nampa, I look more like a Main Coon-especially since I can mimic the pure-bred Main Coons, who are large and perfectly tame."

"You tame? That's a laugh!" Clarence took a jab at Lynx. "I've seen you take swipes at my staff when you aren't happy with what she serves you for breakfast. Underneath your calm exterior, you're a demon."

Lynx lifted a paw up, his pads towards the tabby, jutting out his claws, considering taking a swipe at the feline and then retracted them, "Shut your face! I'm no demon!"

"Whatever!" Clarence rolled his crystal blue eyes. Picking up a paw, shaking it a couple of times, curling his toes, he began cleaning and pretended to ignore the others as they changed the topic.

The little otter stood up on his hind legs, stared into the growing darkness. "Your moon is large tonight. It's so awesome to gaze."

"Why is the night orb orange and larger than normal?" Geoffrey asked.

"Is it important?" Lynx asked.

"It's the Harvest Moon. All Hallow's Eve is next week," Clarence answered, rather bored. He finished with the right paw and lifted the left, shaking it, then curling the toes as he did with the first one and began cleaning it.

"You mentioned that the other day, Clarence. Why is that important?" Lynx asked.

"All Hallow's Eve is the time human kittens dress up as monsters and superheroes to beg for candy and treats. Most important, it is the time spirits with good and evil intention walk the earth looking for mischief.

The ones with good intention will not hurt anyone, though," Clarence stared directly at Lynx. "Your bear god that you don't remember probably has something special planned for you, Lynx. You have a choice, to face this bear god or run away. I have a feeling he will follow you wherever you run to."

The otter smelled the air and wrinkled his nose. "What's the awful smell? Your forest is uninhabitable for a creature like me."

"That's the sugar beet factory," Clarence said, jumping off the doghouse. "Tell me, otter, how are you going to get back home?"

"Not sure. Thought I'd stay here. Where's your lake or river?" the otter turned back to the walking path. "It calls to me. That path. Doesn't it call to you, Lynx?"

"We don't have rivers over here. You need fresh fish or shellfish. We have neither here in the human world. You need to go home," Clarence growled, approaching him in a menacing way.

"I can't. My flight left without me." Wayohm reflected on how the housecat called this the human world as if he was from a different world than them. Weighing it, he pondered on the difference. "You say I'm from a different world than you all because I'm a river otter, from the forest. Perhaps you're right, our habitats are different; but aren't we all still in the world known as Nampa?"

Ignoring the last part of the river otter's statement, Clarence addressed the first part, "Your flight?"

"An eagle brought him," Geoffrey turned. "Clarence, he is our guest. I say we keep him here tonight and Lynx and I can take him back home in the morning."

Crickets chirped their evening song. Wayohm followed Lynx into the doghouse. Lynx covered the little otter up with an extra blanket. He thought about what Clarence said about All Hallow's Eve and the bear god planning something evil for him. He decided not to worry about it. Pushing it out of his mind, he yawned. *Something good had to happen. Well, maybe nothing bad had happened yet. Still, what if what Clarence said is true? Do the animals of the forest celebrate All Hallow's Eve?*

Closing his eyes, he cleared his mind. *That bear god is just an illusion. He can't hurt me.* Gradually, he fell into a peaceful sleep, seeing Tarrier at his anvil hammering a new shield. Then going to his chemicals and herbs to mix a strong potion to anoint the metal for the shield. He heard Tarrier say, *Lynx, this is for you. Protect yourself. Never fear who you really are. Never hide from yourself. I love you and can send more powerful incantations to you through the dimensional portal.*

A bear's roar shattered the peaceful dream. "You can't hide from me, werecat! Come All Hallow's Eve, your hide is mine! Leave this human world! I will find you and destroy you if you don't bow down to me!" Lynx woke with a start, emitting a loud yowl as if hurt. After he recovered his bearings, he said under his breath.

"You send me mixed messages. You say to leave the human world, but you will find me if I do. I don't answer to you. You're not my god!" Lynx responded.

Yet he trembled.

Chapter 7

Wayohm stirred beside Lynx. He felt comforted having the little creature next to him. The bright full moon shone outside, calling Lynx to go out to explore. Carefully, he crept out, hoping to not wake the otter.

Everything appeared different in the dark. He looked up, watching the lazy clouds drift by, briefly covering the moon. Night creatures rubbed their back legs together; their eerie song caused his fur to stand up on end. A slight breeze blew the tree branches and the leaves that were dying rustled, adding to the mystical, chilling sensation traveling up and down the werecat's spine.

Movement by the walking path sparked Lynx's attention. Carefully moving towards it, he wondered if what Geoff said was true. Was there a portal in the middle? He remembered Nickoli, Sarah's Anansi, chanting some type of song. He called it a blessing. Sarah joined in, too. But the language was not English. They called it old Murdoc language that was only used for protection and travel between worlds. Though, Nickoli assured the boys they would not go anywhere once they ended up in the middle. The path had only been done about a week. No one had tried it yet. Then, he noticed there was something moving along the stones, though he couldn't make out what it was.

"Who's there?" Lynx whispered.

"It's me, Wayohm." The little otter answered.

"I left you in the doghouse asleep."

"I came out after you. I'm light on my feet. You don't sleep well. Nightmares cause you to whimper and squirm, preventing me from sleeping well. Come, let's use this walking path to meet the creator you call the only one. What's its name?"

"Albagoth," Lynx answered, walking towards the meditation path. "We need an intention besides seeking Albagoth. Besides, according to Sarah, Albagoth is more about going inside ourselves than seeking outside us," the werecat explained in a low whisper, treading carefully so he didn't step on dry leaves that had fallen from the dogwood tree and the Canadian Maple trees that were in the backyard.

The otter paused at the start of the path, waiting for Lynx. After Lynx reached him, he stood on his back legs, "Let's touch paws and make the same request. That's the same thing as an intention, right?"

Lynx shrugged. "I guess so." Behind him, something crunched the leaves; they jumped. Glancing over their shoulders, they saw Clarence approaching.

"What're you two doing? I'm going to alert Geoffrey to get out here to stop you two," Clarence hissed.

"No, you aren't. I'm going to keep this werecat safe from the bear god. You can either come with us or stay here. And you aren't going to tell that griffin!" Wayohm said sternly.

"Oh yes I am!" Clarence turned around, running full steam towards the cat door, calling behind him, "Speak to the tail!"

"Tattle-tail!" said the otter.

"Ignore him, Wayohm. If we're going to do this, we must do this together, so we don't get separated,"

Lynx held out his paw that was closest to the river otter. Wayohm took it. "Close your eyes and let's agree what to request. Or intend."

Wayohm closed his eyes, "We request to find the true god. Is it Artaois or this Albagoth?"

"Sounds good. Though, Albagoth is inside each of us. Not just outside us," Lynx said. In the back of his mind, Lynx intended to find his true self and a healing for his nightmares. He didn't want to share that with the otter, though. He already knew all paths lead to Albagoth. Even if Artaois has set up to be a god of all wild animals, Lynx refused to bow down to anyone.

They stepped on the first stone. The otter had a harder time reaching the first stone because Lynx's legs were longer than his shorter ones. Lynx asked if he could carry him. The otter refused.

"I got to do this for myself," the otter said proudly. "But we have to get to the middle stone at the same time so we both go through the portal together," Wayohm cautioned.

They jumped. Lynx reached each stone first, letting go of Wayohm's paw at the fourth stone. But he waited for the otter to get there. Then they jumped again. They came to the first path division. They had a choice to go straight across, or veer off the left side or keep going around the circle on the right. If they turned to either the right or the left, they would eventually come to the paths straight across. If they chose to take the first path straight, then they would have to take a jagged right turn until the next left turn that would lead them to the inner stone in the middle of the walking path.

"Which way feels right?" Lynx asked, sensing they needed to go straight. "I say to go straight."

"I think the left way is better," Wayohm offered. "I can't say why."

"If we split up, we might not reach the middle at the same time," Lynx said, visualizing them each landing in different worlds. "We need to stick together."

"Okay. Let's do this. My otter mates, when we're choosing who does something first, we choose a visual object. Choose either a bird, rock, tree or butterfly. If you choose the object I'm thinking of, then we go left. If I choose the object you're thinking of, then we straight. I'm thinking of an object right now. What is it?"

Lynx closed his eyes. What felt right. *I liked to have wings,* he thought, so he said, "Butterfly."

"Ah, no," Wayohm sounded disappointed. "Okay, change items and see if I can choose what you're thinking of."

This time, Lynx choose a tree. He knew trees had good information, and he longed to have a long talk with one. Just not the trees in this world.

The otter put a paw up to his chin as he considered. His whiskers twitched and smiled. "Tree. You're thinking of a tree."

They heard a ruckus coming from inside the Veh house. A light went on in Xander's room. Lynx's heart pounded.

"Come on, we need to rush. Clarence called for back-up. We need to rush this."

They jumped straight to the next stones. The back door opened, Geoffrey came flying out with Xander and Clarence on his back. Xander jumped off just as he saw the river otter and Lynx land on the middle stone and disappear. The last thing Lynx saw was Geoffrey and Clarence flying to the middle stone, calling for them to stop.

Chapter 8

They fell into the void, falling through a swirl of electrified energy and brilliant colors popping and snapping around them. Wayohm yelled, and then laughed. Lynx felt his fur puff out all around him. He wasn't happy at all. Far behind them he heard Clarence screeching as if someone just kicked him in the gut and Geoffrey trying to calm him down.

Wayohm swam to Lynx, "May I have a ride on your back? We should land soon, right?"

"Sure," Lynx held out his arms, "But I'd prefer to hold you, little guy." Wayohm agreed to be held.

"This is fun. It's like sliding down a mud hill into the river. Only we aren't splashing around," Wayohm said with a lilt in his voice.

They landed in a lush forest with strong trees and thick vegetation, like nothing Lynx nor Wayohm ever saw. Lynx landed on his hind legs, because he was holding the river otter. He put the otter down, and Wayohm stood up on his back legs to sniff the air.

"There's a river over to the west. Let's go that way. I'm hungry and my fur needs to be washed." Wayohm dropped down and scampered off. Lynx followed, wishing he had brought his staff from Wayla with him.

They headed out as fast as they could run. Lynx also dropped to all fours to keep up with the river otter. They were far away from where they landed when they both heard Geoffrey and Clarence hit the ground behind them; Clarence let out a blood curdling screech that sounded like someone knocked him out a tree. Lynx chuckled for a bit, even though he knew it was wicked of him to do.

Lynx ran around a shrub, paused to hear the otter splashing and then put the brakes on too fast, sliding into slippery mud, sending him tail over head into the river. While under water, Lynx heard Wayohm and another creature laughing at him. He surfaced and spit out the water, splashing while taking huge gulps of air. He managed to calm down his run-away heart enough to swim to the dry land and crawl out. He shook himself to get most of the water off. Next, he lifted a back leg, bringing it forward, he began to lick it dry. The little otter dove under the water and swam for a bit. When he surfaced, he had an oyster and a rock and began working on it to pry open the shell. Lynx continued licking each part of his body hoping to get the excess water off his fur as much as possible. Then he shook himself again. The sun filtered through the leaves and shrubs, giving the area an interesting glow and shade. He sighed. His stomach rumbled. Turning around, he decided to scan the area for a rabbit.

"The fish are very good," Wayohm suggested as he started pounding on his third oyster shell.

"Are there other fish besides the oysters?" Lynx asked.

"I think so. Are you good at catching them?" the otter asked, flipping the shell open and tossing off the top. He slurped down the slippery flesh inside and licked his lips. "If you don't want to get wet again, I can flip a few up to you." He tossed the bottom shell back in the water and dove in.

Lynx crept closer to the edge, hoping he didn't get splashed. Wayohm flipped up a fish, which kept flapping its tail trying to make its way back to the water, splashing water particles in the werecat's face. He winced. Geoffrey and he went fishing a few days ago and Geoffrey had been the one to pull out the fish with his talons and dropped them in front of him. Lynx remembered helping, but he got splashed more than he was able to catch the slimy little buggers. Still, they managed to bring back a whole slew of them for Erin to fix, overwhelming her.

"Pounce on it!" Wayohm told him, thinking Lynx's reservations were because he didn't know what to do with it. "It won't bite you. This fish has tiny teeth."

Lynx pounced, sinking his claws into the head and body. Finally, it stopped moving so he sat down, grabbed it between his front paws and started gnawing on it. It tasted salty, but it was good. It was better than the fish he and Geoffrey brought home that Erin cooked. It was a treat to have it raw. Wayohm flipped up two more fish and then got out of the water with a couple for himself.

A loud flapping of wings rustled the trees, stirring up the dust and dried grass mixed with the leaves; a screeching of a griffin from above pierced Lynx's quiet meditation on his meal. Lynx and Wayohm scanned the skies to see Geoffrey circling, looking for them. There was a tiny orange and white swirled together spot clinging to the griffin's back, holding on for dear life. Geoffrey let out another sharp screech as he went into a nosedive to land.

"Geoffrey and Clarence found us," Lynx said dryly. "I had hoped they would've landed somewhere else."

"Where's the human that dwells at the house we were at?" Wayohm asked between bites of food.

"Don't know. Maybe he decided to stay at his home. He's decided to become a good student. After his last journey, Sarah and he got together, and she's influenced him to create goals for himself. Not sure what all goes on in his head; Geoffrey is his confidante."

"You feel left out," Wayohm observed.

Lynx shrugged, "Not really." His heart pinged, as another piece of his true self dropped into a deep hole and was covered up. He sighed. It was too dangerous to admit how he felt. He was afraid to admit to himself, too.

Wayohm sensed this. Smiling empathically, "I used to be like you, afraid to admit my hurts and jealousy. I think this griffin and cat accept and love you. If they didn't, they would not have followed us."

Lynx laid his head between his paws to consider. "Maybe. Maybe not. Maybe they're just too nosy to let me do something without them. But how would you know, Wayohm? You aren't very old."

"What I lack in years I made up in heightened knowing or intuition, as that griffin calls it. I hear the voice within guiding and directing me. I don't know what to call it. I just follow it," Wayohm answered.

Geoffrey and Clarence trotted over, hearing the last words. "We don't want you to get in trouble," Geoffrey said.

"We're concerned about you. Xander, Milo and Sarah didn't even realize that the walking path they created is a portal. Xander knows now that he saw us disappear through the middle stone. We wanted to stop you two and let the humans try it out first."

"Fat chance of that! Xander renounced going on adventures until after the Sage of Stillness trains him," Lynx spat.

"Oh, shut up!" Geoffrey snapped. "I don't know where you got that idea! You've been one sour werecat for a week or more. Look, we're in wherever we are and we will face these nightmares with you, Lynx. Deal with it!"

Lynx pouted. "I have not! Geoff!"

"Really? You've been pouting around, acting tough and refusing to talk to anyone, while we all hear your whimpers and yelps whenever you fall asleep. While you're awake, you mope, saying you aren't appreciated!" Geoffrey yelled.

"We're all pampered at the Veh house!" Clarence added his two cents. "And if our staff knew there was a river otter living with us, she'd ask her mate to put in a small pond for him. She'd probably get fish to put in it, too."

"I don't want to stay at your holt," Wayohm said softly. "I was just there because it was too late to get back to mine with my mom, pa and siblings. Look, we have bigger problems, right now. We don't know where we are. I'm not even sure this is the world we came from."

Geoffrey lifted his head and sniffed. "We aren't in the World of Nampa anymore," he said dryly. "Come on, let's walk to see if we can find someone to tell us where we are." Geoffrey started walking away from the river. Clarence followed.

"This place looks normal," Lynx protested. "Maybe that portal is just a shortcut to the wilderness we hunt in." He remained steadfast where he was, head in paws, his paws resting on a partially eaten fish.

"It isn't. The shellfish here taste different than back home. Didn't you notice that in the fish I gave you, Lynx?" said Wayohm.

"No, not really. Usually fish tastes salty. This one tasted more peppery and spiced up." Lynx thought about it, replaying his words. "I supposed I just agreed with you, Wayohm."

Lynx lifted his head, wondering why the otter didn't answer; he saw him scampering after Geoffrey and Clarence. He let out a frustrated sigh. Maybe he should just stay here and feel sorry for himself.

A loud crack from a nearby tree startled him. Then a high pitch, "Oooo, eeee, aaaah" rose out of the shrubs behind him. "He's coming for you, werecat. Beware! Artaois will find you!"

"Hey, wait up!" Lynx jumped to his feet and ran as fast as he could to catch up.

Morning mist rose from the forest bed. Large paws stomped through dry leaves, not caring who woke up as the bulky grizzly lumbered to his altar, growling and laughing whenever a smaller creature ran away from him, shrieking, "Beware! Artaois is angry!"

The fox stood by the large cauldron, holding a thick book, grinning. "I'm your humble servant, Lord Artaois," he bowed when the bear got there.

"Knock it off, Pentaham. You know I hate kiss-butt creatures!"

"Yes, Lord Artaois. Whatever you say. You're angry today. How may I help you punish the one that upset you?"

The massive bear god roared loudly. "I will take care of him and all who dare helped him escape me! That werecat will pay for the day an outsider saved his hide from the flames! He will burn again and this time completely!"

The fox smiled, "Yesss, Lord Artaois. He'll be a crispy critter."

"Leave my sight! I hate kiss-butts!" Artaois back handed him, knocking him off the boulder he stood on so that he dropped the book. "If you come back here, I will roast you alive and feed you to my cubs!"

The fox scampered off.

Artaois bent down, picked up the book, stood, turned around and sat on the boulder. Opening the heavy book, he started thumbing through it looking for the enchantments necessary to divine where Lynx went to.

The early morning sun rose above the meadow, the light bouncing off a clear, round object. The bear looked up at it to see it was a perfectly polished quartz crystal ball.

"Well, hello, there. I heard about you. I've never seen you before." Artaois put the book down, bent over and picked up the ball in his large paw. As he stared at it, he could see minor fractures inside that looked like they formed images and words. On impulse, he asked a question, "Where is that blasted werecat?"

The lines moved, which amazed the bear. He'd never seen anything like that. It formed the words, "In his own world. The one you came from, too."

"I knew that werecat wasn't in the right world. But this is my world."

"Then where are your parents?" The lines said.

"How do I know? They sent me away when I was young. All bear parents send their young away . . ." Artaois closed his eyes, swaying backward as he vaguely remembered falling through a hole in the ground before he was old enough to be on his own. "Do you know where I came from?"

"No," the quartz ball spelled out.

"Hold it, you changed the topic to me. It's that damn werecat I need to know about. Do you know where Lynx is?" the bear went back to his original concern.

"No, I don't. Even if I did, I wouldn't tell you."

"Hmm. I need someone who can give me more information. Not just where Lynx is, but how I can find him."

"You can't," said a voice behind him. Artaois turned to see the largest cat he had ever seen. The feline stood at least five feet from the shoulder to his front paws, pure white fur with black spots, short ears with long tufts, large paws used for climbing steep mountains and snowy/icy areas and a medium stubby tail. He also had fluffy cheek fur.

"I haven't seen you in my woods before. Who are you? And where did you come from?"

"I'm Manx, a Snowshoe Lynx. I'm a spiritual guide apprentice and travel to many worlds. I'm here to warn you to stay away from Lynx the werecat. He's a lot of things, mischief maker, shapeshifter and most of all, he hides his true form, but he has a good heart and soul. You make trouble for him and I will see that you meet Albagoth in person. Do you understand me?"

"Albagoth?" Artaois laughed loud and heartedly. "What kind of a name is that?"

"Albagoth is the Creator of All Worlds. A living spirit that dwells within all plants, rocks and trees, animals and humans. You say you are the god of this world . . ."

"I am the god of the forest animals. Most werecats know of me and stay hidden, like bigfoot. I warn them to stop trusting humans and they listen to me. This one stray werecat won't listen to me."

"There aren't werecats in this world, so how can you rule them?" Manx pointed out.

"They are here. It's just they're hiding from me," the bear felt a ping deep in his being, as his face flushed, lowering his head; he knew he was lying. But he wished what he said was true. If humans believed the Yeti was hiding from them, then why can't werecats be hiding from him, a bear god who would demand their obedience?

Artaois shifted his weight from one front paw to the other, muttering softly to himself as he thought. Shrugging, "I don't know. All I do know is Lynx has to stay away from humans! They tormented him once and will again. If he doesn't listen, then I have to hurt him and blame them!"

"How do you know humans have hurt him in the past?" Manx sat down, patiently waiting for his answer, knowing that the bear couldn't answer this.

Artaois took a deep breath, raised his head up to sky, scanning the clouds, wondering why no one believed him. Shrugging once more, lowering his head, his eyes filled with doubt and hurt, "I don't know. It's just a vague knowing. Humans roam these woods hurting, killing so many of my animals. . ."

"Then why single Lynx out?"

Artaois weighed the words carefully. "Because he appears vulnerable, innocent and I want to protect him. But if he won't listen to reason, I have to hurt him."

"No, you won't," Manx replied empathically, sitting down.

"You plan to stop me?" the massive bear stood up to his full height.

The Snowshoe Lynx growled, "I'm not afraid of you, Artaois. I've heard of you. We've studied your legends and wrote some of our own to entertain other children in other worlds. I am Lynx's protector. You will leave him alone or you will suffer the consequences."

Manx turned and left. Artaois stood there, mulling over what the snowshoe lynx said. It bothered him not knowing who the animal was working with. He wanted to know. Only he was the all-knowing god of this forest. But he couldn't see who this lynx was and who he worked with.

"Who do you work with?" the bear said ten minutes after that snow lynx left. Then it struck him; if he was all knowing, why didn't he know where Lynx went and how he got there? He went down to his front feet, hearing his stomach growl loudly. He growled back at it. Berries sounded good, so he went in search of a berry bush and maybe some fish. While there, he wanted to check up on that pesky otter, Wayohm, who kept defending the werecat.

While at the river, he spotted many otters playing in the water, feasting on fish or tossing pebbles back and forth to each other. None looked like Wayohm.

"Hey, otters, I'm looking for someone. Can you help me find him?"

"Oh no! It's that bear that claims to be a god," one of the otter pups whispered.

"Should we run? Or answer his questions?" another otter pup, with lighter brown fur and a strip of white fur down her head asked.

"No, he'll just splash in and chase us," the first answered.

"I'm looking for an otter. I think his name is Wayohm. He likes to hang out near my altar stones, spying on me and my assistants. Do you know where he is?"

"Why do you want to know?" an older otter sow asked. "These are my pups. You better talk to me."

"Someone I'm putting a hex – ahem- I mean— someone I'm trying to help has disappeared and Wayohm seemed concerned for this animal's welfare. I want to know if he knows what happened to this animal because he might be in danger."

"The animal in question is in danger from you," An adult male otter, called a boar, spoke up, strolling out from the bushes. "We won't tell you where Wayohm is."

"We don't know where Wayohm is. He's near adulthood. He's my sister's boy. We take care of him because my sister and her boar were killed. He won't answer to us and doesn't tell us where he got up," said the sow who was just coming out of the water. "Come on, kids, let's go to our holt." She swam to dry land. The kids followed.

One of the otter pups paused and turned to Artaois, "I saw Wayohm going deeper in the forest. I followed him to where the large snowy owl nests. Next thing I know, a large eagle picked him up and carried him off. I think Wayohm became food for the eaglets."

"Jasper! That isn't a nice thing to say about your uncle!"

"But, Mom, Wayohm doesn't listen to you or Grandma and Granddad. He plays with any animal, even ones that might turn on him and eat him. It serves him right!"

"Jasper! Go to your holt room and stay there--think about what you just said."

"Aw, Mom!" Jasper protested.

"That isn't nice! Jasper! Uncle Wayohm is thoughtful, inquisitive and protective of others! He better not be eagle food!" said his sister.

"Listen to your mom, Jasper!" said his dad.

"Yes, Dad." The little otter hung his head and scampered to the burrow.

"Thank you, Jasper," Artaois said. Turning, he stalked off, setting his mind to finding the snowy owl.

"If that owl admits to anything, I will show him who is boss in these woods," the bear god growled under his breath. "I rule these woods. Next order of business is to find out what is blocking me from being all knowing and all seeing. I knew everything before that damn werecat disappeared!"

The sky drew dark as storm clouds rolled in. Thunder boomed over the distant mountains; the bear growled back at it. "I should be able to tame this oncoming storm. Curse you, weather gods! Let me have my way or else!"

"Or else what?" a voice called from a tree above Artaois. He paused and gazed upward.

"Who are you? Reveal yourself!" demanded the impatient god.

"I'm the one who says "Who" around these parts. This is my territory, bear. I'm Mylar. I heard you were looking for me," the Snowy Owl came out of the dark pine tree branches to show himself in the fast disappearing sunlight.

"I rule these woods, Snowy Owl! I'm the bear god who protects all woodland creatures," Artaois bellowed.

"We'll see about that. What do you want with me?" Mylar replied.

"You helped a young river otter. I want to know what you told him and where he went."

"What I told him is between him and me. I don't reveal secrets. You think you're an all-knowing god, so tell me why it is you are so interested in hurting a werecat that hasn't hurt you?" Mylar asked.

"How did you know this is about that werecat?"

"I observe all that goes on in this forest as I sleep. I've seen you dancing under the light of the moon, saying your enchantments and making your potions. Others stay away except those who claim to worship you out of fear. Those who stand up to you act on their strength. Now, answer my question."

"He's playing with humans. He's been hurt before. He ignores me..."

"He remembers nothing about you, Artaois or your ancestors. He doesn't recognize your godly hood. Neither do I! In fact, most animals of this forest follow a spiritual path their heart directs them. You are a bully who intimidates other animals to bow down to you. No god or creator I am aware of would treat their creations in that manner," the snowy owl instructed.

"What do you know of being a god?" Artaois demanded.

"I know a creator would love their creations and assist them in ways of understanding. If you are so all-knowing, you tell me what I told the young river otter?" The owl's large yellow eyes looked through the grizzly bear's eyes to see the soul Artaois wasn't aware he had.

Artaois snarled. Closing his eyes, clearing his mind, he focused on trying to locate the otter. He saw Lynx and a smaller animal, which appeared larger than he remembered the otter to be, landing on a small stone in the center of a strange stone path in the backyard of a human. A bright, swirling light erupted from that stone and swallowed the two animals followed by a griffin and a common house cat. He exhaled gruffly. "They went through an opening in a stone. I don't know what that means. Is it symbolic for something else?"

"You amaze me, Artaois. For a bear who wants to be a god, you are just learning how to answer your own questions. The secret to finding the true creator is through meditation and looking within. Learn compassion. Once you do, you will see a world of difference."

The bear hung his head, remembering how he shooed the otter away and how he snarled at his assistant. "I really haven't hurt anyone, Mylar. I just don't have patience. . ."

The Owl screeched, not allowing the self-appointed bear god to finish his sentence. "Then why are you inflicting nightmares on the werecat?"

"How do you know about that?" The bear was surprised.

"I have my spies and my own wisdom. I fly at night. My spirit flies while I sleep in the day. I see more when asleep than I do when awake. I've spotted the griffin and werecat here hunting and listen to them. They are from another world. A world you know nothing of. They live with friends who happen to be human and they will protect those humans with their lives, if they have to."

Artaois' shoulders and head sagged. He wanted to crawl under a bush and disappear. "You're wise. But why tell me this?"

"To give you an insight into their world and why they are in ours. Leave them alone. Or you will be the one suffering severe consequences. Your spells will backfire. You may leave my presence now. This is daytime. I must sleep!" The owl turned his back to the grizzly bear and closed his eyes.

Well, if that isn't a slap in the face! Artaois turned around, fuming inwardly. *Stupid featherbrain. Now what do I do? Might as well head back to my altar and think. Maybe that stone I found has some direction for me.*

The massive grizzly made his way through the thick vegetation, small insects buzzing around him. Above, an eagle called, and a hawk answered. Small critters scampered out of his way. He paused to sniff the air. Smaller birds fled the bushes, causing the bear to jump, not expecting the flight. He considered the words of the snowshoe lynx. Gods don't want to be feared, but all he knew was animals feared him.

"I'm all powerful!" Artaois roared once he made it into an open meadow. "Snowshoe lynx, if you are still around here, come back and face me. I have questions for you! One, you alluded to working with someone, who do you work with?" The air was still. All animals grew quiet. The bear listened to the crackling under his large, black pot.

The shrubs moved as if a slight breeze moved them. Artaois' fur stood on end as a bolt of lightning struck a tree about a yard away from him. A large black cloud opened its doors and poured down, extinguishing the fire under the kettle, setting a nearby bush on fire. Manx stepped out of the burning bush, unharmed.

"You summoned me. I'm not a genie, Artaois," Manx said dryly. "You talked to the owl. You have questions and concerns?"

The bear turned around to face the snowshoe lynx. "Yes. I demand to know who you work with."

"You aren't in any shape to demand anything of me, though, my partner says to be honest with you. I work with a human who has been granted immortality. He travels to all worlds and helps those who request it.

He, though, is not to interfere with animals, such as yourself, unless asked and if that animal also is working with humans. You are prejudiced against humans, so he won't interfere in this. Lynx must find his own way. And you need to find your own way. I've covered this with you. I've also told you to stay away from Lynx."

The bear turned around, mulling over his words. "Humans preys on us animals, killing us for sport. I have my reasons to hate them. I must warn Lynx. I have his best interest at heart. Don't you see?"

"No, I don't see. Not all humans are like those that choose to prey on wild animals for sport. There are good humans that save and work to protect all life on their worlds, recognizing the consciousness inside of each living being," Manx said, walking around to face the bear. "Right now, Lynx could be in danger. He's in a world he knows nothing about. All because you chased a little river otter away who was questioning you bewitching a werecat and that little otter has convinced Lynx to jump through a portal that they don't know where it leads to. I'll blame you if anything happens to either one of them."

Artaois gulped hard, imagining something tragic happening to them. "If I am responsible, then how can I help? Where is this portal?"

"It is a symbol that a human female brought back from her birth world. The boys who created the walking path changed it, a bit, though. You will find it in a human backyard. Are you sure you want to go there? You might get shot," Manx sneered.

"You're daring me to go, aren't you?"

"I'm daring you to prove your godhood, Artaois. I'm daring you to do the right thing."

"How do I get there?" Artaois repeated.

"By following me. I have a way to transport you there. But I won't follow unless you want me to." Manx offered. "I'll give you the day and one night to consider." Manx turned to walk back the way he came. Lightning struck ahead, lighting up the way. Thunder rumbled.

Artaois grumbled, stamping his right foot, causing the ground around him to shake. "You think you're so high and mighty! You act like you're the god and I'm the mindless creation! I hate depending on you! You, you," he fumbled for words, while going over to his black cauldron. He started kicking dirt around the fire, as his thoughts swirled on how to get where Lynx was. He'd never traveled to another world before. He couldn't visualize what that world had for him. Depending on this strange snowshoe lynx would make him weak if other forest creatures saw him asking for help. His other option would be to find a way to get to this human's house without being seen.

Once the fire was out, the grizzly bear sat down, and yawned. He hadn't slept in a long time. That werecat frightened him more than the snowshoe lynx. Closing his eyes, he laid down to sleep. His mind traveled back to that river otter's question, "Why are you so frightened of the werecat?"

Artaois snapped at him rather than answer. He remembered the river otter mentioned a griffin as did the snow owl. Why hadn't he been concerned about the griffin, the river otter asked.

"Griffins aren't real." Artaois said out loud to himself. "If I did see them hunting, I thought it was a large dog with the werecat. It was an odd pairing." Maybe a glamor was on the griffin. He laughed softly. "Preposterous! Humans don't know how to put glamor on mythical creatures! Besides, griffins aren't real. That otter and owl are mistaken!"

Artaois' mind traveled to his cubhood. The sky appeared to be violet with an orange tinge. He sat between his parents, eating and looking around at everything else. A clear form floated over him, a young werecat, looking frightened and injured. He remembered saying to his parents that the cub was dead and his spirit had to be sent to the great beyond. His dad back pawed him, saying werecats were demons and didn't have souls. His pa reminded him that they, the bears, were the gods. His eyes flew open, "That wasn't in this world. Where was it? How would I know this?" he yawned. "Maybe I'll have to revisit this," he mumbled as his eyes closed again. He curled into a ball.

Artaois saw himself falling in a circle as if he was being sucked down a whirlpool at the end of a waterfall. Emerging into the bright sunlight, sparkling like a star – brighter than any star he'd ever seen- he took a deep breath of fresh air. Spotting land not far away, he swam towards it and crawled out. Once on land, he shook himself. A massive shadow blocked out the sun, shielding him from the heat he hoped to dry himself by. Glancing up, the massive grizzly shrunk away. A bear twenty feet tall and wider than him many times over stood in front of him.

"Who are you?" The shadow growled. Artaois let out a whimper.

"I-I-I- um" he stuttered, wishing the words would come faster.

"Spit it out, bear!"

"Um, I'm trying."

"Do or not! There is no try!" The massive bear roared. "I know who you are. I want to hear you say it!"

"Artaois, the bear god of the forests."

The other bear roared with laughter that shook the wilderness.

"You call yourself a bear god? If you were truly a god, you could transport yourself anywhere you chose to be! You would also be aware griffins are real. There is one in your midst that is a very powerful being of good. You dare harm their friends and you will incur their wraith!"

"Um, I, okay – I guess. But if I may, who are you?" Artaois stammered.

"We are the Creator of All Worlds! I go by many names. The one you are threatening calls me Albagoth!"

Artaois woke up, panting and sweating, uncurled his form and stretched out. Rolling over, he decided to go down to the river to get a drink and wake up a bit. That dream was frightening.

On the way down to river, the dream replayed over and over, each time, his heart skipped a beat at the size of the other bear. Once at the river, he took a deep, long drink. After he got his fill, he licked and smacked his lips, deciding it was just a dream. "My mind is just using all that I learned yesterday to frighten me. Griffins aren't real, and this other god is mistaken. But I must consider how to transport myself like that lynx cat does."

Artois jumped in the river, watching for a fish to swim by. Just as he pounced on one, he heard the shrubs rustle and dry leaves crunching under footsteps. He missed the fish he was aiming for; instead, he got a mouthful of water that tasted horrible.

"What did you decide?" Manx asked as he strolled out.

The bear god turned around, to see the snowshoe lynx standing there, grinning at him. He turned around to see who spoke to him.

"I'll go with you," the bear said, water dripping from his jaws.

"Are you ready to go?" Manx said.

"No! I haven't had my breakfast! I'm so hungry, I could eat half my subjects!"

"A true god wouldn't need to eat, Artaois." Manx sneered.

"Grrr!" Artaois waddled out of the water, shook himself off. "I'm a physical god, Manx. You weren't supposed to come until I summon you. I haven't summoned you!"

"I'm not a genie, need I remind you? I answer to my own internal guidance. You need to go now before the portal changes directions. If we wait too long, we may end up in a different world than where Lynx and the others are," Manx replied.

The massive grizzly's stomach roared. "I must eat something!"

"Fine!" Manx saw a rabbit or two hopping out of their burrow, pausing to look at Manx. Artaois noticed the rabbits standing up on their hind legs, whiskers trembling and noses twitching. They exchanged glances at each other and nodded their consent. Manx thanked them and then pounced on them, killing them instantly with no fight. He tossed the bodies to the bear. "Here you go. These two agreed to be your food source. You're welcome."

The bear cocked his head, curious, "What do you mean they agreed to feed me?"

"We always ask the animals for permission to feed us. If they say no, then we move on. We respect all life, Artaois. Now eat fast. That portal is constantly changing."

The bear ate his rabbits in two bites. "Now, how do we get there?"

"Put one of your paws on my shoulder," Manx said. The bear did as he was told. Manx balanced on three feet, lifting the fourth front up and turning a nob on a gadget on the wrist of his other front paw. They disappeared and reappeared in the Veh's backyard.

A man dressed in a maroon robe with a hood stood in the middle of the yard. He took down his hood briefly, revealing his dark face, long black hair and green eyes. He smiled at Manx. Around his neck was a symbol of a fire, but Artaois couldn't make out what was burning. He walked over to Manx, taking off the symbol and handed it to Manx.

"Give this charm to Lynx when you see him. It will change shape once Lynx finds his true self," the man said.

"Yes, Sage Tomás." Manx said. The Sage took off the vortex watch from Manx's wrist. "You will get home without this. Albagoth guides you. Remember to seek within. Now go!"

Manx nodded, "Yes, Sage. Thank you." He turned to the bear, "Come, let's go."

In one jump, they landed on the center stone which sucked them in.

Chapter 9

Lynx strutted out in front, doing his best to be the brave leader, though he knew not where they were going or where they were. Wayohm scampered up to him, "Where are you leading us?"

"Somewhere," Lynx stated confidently. His shoulders sagged. In the distance, he heard a whimper, sob and cry for help. He paused. "Do you hear that?"

Perking his ears up, he swiveled them around like satellite antennas to tune where the cries were coming from. Lynx saw a figure huddled on the ground up on a distant hillside.

"Look, over there! Do you see it?" He lifted a paw up and pointed.

"No, I don't hear or see anything," Wayohm said. He turned to Geoffrey and Clarence, who came up last.

"What's up?" Geoffrey asked.

"Lynx hears and sees something. I can't see anything except lots of green, lush meadow and trees. I smell fresh air, too. Not like back home with the human smog that drifts up to us," Wayohm declared.

Geoffrey squinted. "Hmm." He scanned the distance and then looked closer at Lynx.

"How long has it been since you got a good night's sleep, Lynx?"

"What does that have to do with anything? There's a creature who is in distress! We need to go help him!" Lynx bellowed.

Geoffrey exchanged worried looks with Clarence, who nodded at him as if to say, "Go ahead. Be brave."

"My Grandsire the healer said if a person, griffin or any animal goes without good sleep, they start seeing and hearing things that aren't there. I'm concerned about you."

Lynx jutted his chin out. "I'm not going crazy, if that's what you are inferring! I see something and hear the cries! It's real and I will show you!" The werecat sat back on his hunches, lifted his front paws and snapped his thumbs against the first toes on both paws, disappearing and reappearing on the hillside.

Once on the hillside, Lynx sniffed the ground and the air, perked his ears and followed a scent. He noticed there wasn't the putrid smell like back home that accompanied his nightmares and other times he heard the cries and pleas for help. He shook his head. There wasn't a creature huddled up under blankets like he saw. Taking a deep breath, he let it out abruptly in one 'swoosh!'"

Okay, Albagoth, guide me. What I am doing here? Why am I hearing cries for help? Show me how to help myself. Maybe Geoff is right. Maybe I'm losing my mind?

A small voice answered him, *No, you aren't. Find the town. Look for others that look like you. Watch out for anything that doesn't belong.*

Lynx nodded to the voice, to show he understood. He sighed, stood up and started walking up the hill. At this point, he just wanted to be alone. He realized this was his journey and he needed to go alone. Though, he knew his friends cared and wanted to help, he wasn't sure how they could.

Lynx's three friends watched Lynx stroll up the hill. "Shouldn't we go after him?" Wayohm and Clarence asked.

Geoffrey shook his head, "He needs to do this alone. But we are going to follow him from a distance. We need to make it so he believes his is alone. But we will be there if anything happens and he needs our assistance," Geoffrey glanced at both. "I have a sense that Lynx is following his inner guidance right now. Come on, let's take to the sky." He lowered himself and the other two climbed on. "Hang on with your claws, but not too deep. I need to get a harness to strap you two in." The albino griffin ran a few feet, flapped his long, strong wings and jumped into the air.

Artaois and Manx landed in the lush jungle with tropical birds of many sizes and sounds of chirping, cawing and warbling. Squirrels, ground rodents and rabbits scurried around. Pausing to consider where they could be, something familiar struck Artaois; half closing his eyes, he could visualize a den somewhere in the mountains not far from here. Though, he didn't know how he knew. The other animals and birds quieted themselves, while they ran to their burrows. The bear smiled, but a sadness descended on him, which he quickly stuffed deep down.

Manx noticed, being trained to observe his student's responses. He wished the other animals weren't so quick to run.

Opening his eyes, Artaois noticed the sunlight filtered through the leaves, casting shadows and light –he marveled at the rainbow colors that he hadn't seen anywhere before except after a rainstorm back home. Once out in the open, he paused and looked up at the sky, noticing it was orange with purple clouds floating by. A few of the clouds appeared to be making pirouettes or spinning gracefully across the sky. Others lengthened themselves out and glided like a human figure skater. The bear had witnessed humans skating on frozen waters out in the woods. When they cleared, he tried it, but ended up with his four feet going every which way before he tumbled hind-end overhead and skidded on his back to rest against a tree on the bank. All the animals who watched laughed at him. He sighed, then looked back up at the sky noticing the sun was also bright pink with shades of deep brown. Manx turned around to see where his student was.

"It's awesome, isn't it?" Manx observed.

"What is awesome?" Artaois looked at him.

"How Albagoth created so many different worlds and each new world I visit has a sun that is different from the others. The creator knows beauty and keeps all healthy, inspired and shows us how to find our way."

Artaois' heart dropped down to his stomach. Lowering his head to hide his hurt, he considered what to say. "Albagoth again. He's the creator. What does that make me?"

"Albagoth is nether male nor female. It makes you a mighty strong bear with a lot of wisdom, but you don't know how to use it. You are chosen to be here right now, a bear created by the imagination of Albagoth, yet you haven't found what you need."

"Why can't this Albagoth come down to face me?" the bear growled.

Manx let out a chuckle, shaking his head from side to side. Lifting his head, he looked his student in the eye, "Albagoth gives all free will to find their own path. Albagoth doesn't demand worship nor desire to be celebrated. Guidance comes from within. Not from without."

The bear shrugged his massive shoulders. "I rule by intimidation! Other animals are afraid of me! That is my power."

"Do you like them to run from you? Wasn't there a time when you wanted the other animals to accept you, be friends with you, and you longed to help them and be helped in return?"

Artaois turned his back to his teacher, vividly recalling a time as a cub new to the World of Nampa, as the humans called it. A cub with tan fur with black spots came out to greet him. The youngster was about his age, and Artaois wanted to ask the cub where he was. The cub said he was a Mountain lion cub and offered to play. Then the mom came out and grabbed her cub by the nape and ran away. Artaois remembered following them at a safe distance to see them go towards a den in a cave. Before going in, the mom put her cub down and he heard the mom say, "That's a bear. He might be a cub, but he's dangerous. He could kill you with one bite to your throat. Stay away from him."

Those words hurt him, and the memory still bothered him. He only wanted to know where he was and how to survive in a land so new to him.

Artaois decided the other animals running from him gave him power. His parents said they were the gods, so not to be afraid. Men tried to kill his momma; instead his dad came up and overpowered them. He remembered how his parents mauled those hunters. As a cub, Artaois knew his parents weren't the bad guys. Those men would have killed his momma. So, he figured they were the bad guys.

But there was this young werecat he remembered seeing chasing after young humans, as if they were his saviors. Artaois remembered trying to save the young werecat, who looked fierce, yet naïve. But he wouldn't listen. The next thing he knew, the boys turned on him, chasing him under a wooden cart and it was on fire. Artaois remembered trying to help, but his parents prevented him.

"It's his own fault . . ." his poppa said.

"I'm a Grizzly bear. We're supposed to live alone and have few friends. Only when we mate, and then the fathers don't have anything to do with the cubs," he drew out his words in a thoughtful tone. Glancing up at his teacher, "I never wanted friends. Yet there are little creatures who gather around me, wanting to please me in hopes I won't eat them. I shoo them away. I don't need minions."

Artaois turned back to the path and walked on, not waiting for Manx to lead the way.

"You had a poppa," Manx said as they strolled.

"I have vague memories of it, but on the world we came from, male and female bears don't stay together." He paused to consider. "Everyone says I came from the same land as Lynx. Maybe I did. There was this hole I fell through as I was trying to protect that young werecat. Poppa said I was too soft hearted. . ."

"What happened to make you turn hard hearted?" Manx asked. Before the grizzly could answer, they heard a beast lumbering through the forest. Manx and Artaois paused to look. They both smelled the air.

"It smells like a bear," Artaois said. Scanning the landscape, he and Manx tightened their muscles, preparing for fight or flight in case the approaching bear wasn't receptive to them being here.

Manx sniffed the nearby bushes and vegetation to get a better idea of whose territory they were in. Shaking his head, he said, "This isn't that bear's territory. It belongs to another animal that I can't identify."

Artaois relaxed a bit, sniffed the same places he observed Manx visit. "Werecat territory. There has to be a den around here somewhere." Manx nodded, agreeing.

A bear came into view. It was a medium build, though, still massive, black bear. It stopped, cocked its head, as if questioning what it was seeing. Then it smiled.

"Artaois? Is that you?" it asked, its eyes twinkling with recognition. "I thought the Ohanaians got you. You disappeared after you went chasing that werecub so many years ago. You never listened to Momma or Poppa."

Artaois' jaw dropped. "Who are you?" he asked, once he found his voice.

The other bear's face registered hurt. "I'm your sister. Don't you remember me?" Artaois shook his head, trying to remember her.

"I was an only cub," he replied slowly. "But I don't remember much."

"I'm Annilia. I was about an hour ahead of you. What happened to you?"

"Annilia," Artaois raised a paw up and scratched his head, then shrugged. "I can't place much. It was a long time ago."

"Five or six years. You ran off chasing some young werecats. One in particular because you were afraid for it heading into the Ohanian village." Annilia sat down, smiling, remembering something. "Can you still start fires by rubbing your front paws together?"

Artaois' was at a loss for words, *I used to start fires by rubbing my paws together?* He sat down, amazed. "I don't remember doing that," he said slowly.

Manx sat off in the distance, listening to the two siblings chatting, wondering what insight he could bring into the discussion.

"Yeah, you did. You used to watch the Ohanians start fires to cook their food. You were impressed, so said we need to cook our food, too. You knew we were gods, so you created fire with your paws. Momma and Poppa mauled two Ohanaian hunters, you started the fire with the wood they gathered and we cooked their limbs. It was good. But after you disappeared, we couldn't start fires. Momma and Poppa never learned how you did that." She paused to walk closer to him. "It's been a lean several years here. But you look healthy and well fed. Where have you been? What happened to you?"

"I've been able to find food easily enough in the world I came from." Artaois followed the strange female bear as she circled him. "I don't know what happened. I vaguely remember falling through a hole and landing in a place where I couldn't find Momma and Poppa. . ." She stepped closer and inhaled his scent, then backed away, repulsed.

"Wherever you were, sure has an awful scent. What kind of weird trees were there?"

Manx's eyes flew open, clearing his throat to get attention, "Um, hey, Annilia, where are we? You called the people here Ohanaians."

"Yeah – Ohanaians- People of the land. This world is Ohana. The Land," she replied without thinking. Narrowing her eyes, she examined the snowshoe lynx, "You're not a werecat. Who are you and where are you from?"

"No, I'm not a werecat. I'm a snowshoe lynx from another world that Albagoth has created. The name of it isn't important to you at this time."

"I'll be the judge of that," she sneered. "Alba-whoey? If that is some other known creator garbage, you're sadly mistaken. Us bears are the only gods here, though the Ohanaians don't recognize us. They say all are one and so on. We know better. They have tried to kill us, when that doesn't work, they run away. All the creatures here respect us, and we try to care for them. Except werecats. They follow their own laws and bow down to no one. I believe all feline species are part werecats," Annilia said, lifting her head up and jutting out her chin. "Come, follow me. Momma and Poppa will want to see you. They'll be glad to know you are safe and back home."

Manx shook his head, replaying Annilia's words about all felines being part werecat. Shrugging, he asked, "What do you know about werecats?"

"They can change their form. Some can shift into Ohanaian if they choose – pretending to be someone they aren't. Some choose their Ohanaian shape that is distinctly different than any of the Ohanaians in the village. Some become other animals to blend in. But around here, if a werecat dares to do any of that, and they are discovered, they are called demons and the Ohanaians will forbid them to be in the village." Annilia scanned the ground, pausing. "We're in werecat territory. But they're hiding from us. Some are afraid of us bears because they know we outclass them. They're lowlife scum."

Manx harrumphed.

"What's wrong, snowshoe lynx?" she turned to him, glaring fiercely at him. "Don't believe me? Just wait till you meet one face-to-face!" She growled.

They continued in silence, she led them over a hill and through a winding path that followed a river. Down below, Manx observed Lynx and the others by the river. He hoped Lynx stayed hidden for a while until he could sort out what to do with Artaois and this new family.

As they walked, Artaois thought about what he was learning of his kind. If this was the world he was born in, then what was he to do? If he could create fire with his paws, then why couldn't he still do that? Mostly, he had hoped he could learn what plants and herbs were here that he could use to continue to cast enchantments on Lynx to lure him away from the humans. Or cause him to see that humans were the evil ones. But how? And if werecats were a law unto themselves, then that explained why Lynx didn't follow his godship.

Annilia turned a sharp corner that headed up a steep mountain. Manx and Artaois saw that it plateaued as it led to an entrance of a cave. It reminded Manx of the cave where Manitor lived in Curá. But it was different, because there were a few trees and the plateau went around it. The trio headed up the steep slope, with smaller rocks that were loose, dislodging and tumbling down. Two large grizzlies came out of the cave to watch them climb up. Both had greying muzzles.

Artaois paused when he saw them, awed by the sight of his parents.

"Momma? Poppa?" he uttered. The two nodded, shocked. He broke into an unsteady run, passing the bear who claimed to be his sister. Once on top, he embraced both parents one at a time.

"Arty, where have you been? It's been four years since you vanished," his momma stated.

"Don't worry about that, Mildred," the father said. "He's back just in time to meet Annilia's mate and celebrate the coming of her cubs in a few months. Come in, come in," he stated. Then the father noticed Manx and his eyes narrowed. "But not you, werecat. We don't allow your kind around us," he growled.

"I'm not a werecat," Manx said between gasping breaths as he finished the long climb. "I'm a snowshoe lynx that isn't from your world."

"Ha! This is the only world, you fool! The only kind of feline here are demon werecats! They can pose as anything. I banish you in the name of the mighty Artaois the First!"

"Who?" Manx sat down, cocking his head. "You're saying your son was the first?"

"Byomens, no! My son was named for the first creator grizzly this world has ever known. We continue his legacy and honor all he taught us. Artaois the First knew there had to be others to walk this Ohana – so he created all creatures- squirrels, foxes, birds and lizards- to live on it. Then he created other bears to rule them, teaching them how to be the overseers," the father said. "But you were raised here, so surely you know the stories."

"No, I don't. I'm from a different world, like I said."

"Artaois the First didn't create other worlds. That's a myth and heresy against our godhood," the elder bear growled. "You could be mauled at moonrise if you don't renounce that!"

"Now, Arnold, remember werecats have their own rules. They don't recognize us as their rightful gods. Just let the poor mistaken fool go," the elder female bear said and lightly tapped her mate's shoulder. "Besides, Arty just returned to us. We must call the scribe to come. Sit by the fire tonight so we can add to the histories. We will call our neighbors to come for the feast."

Artaois didn't know what to say, he turned to look at Manx and said lowly, "You better go. Find Lynx. Remind him that when I find him, I will not be forgiving. I'm still out to make his life miserable."

Manx grimaced. Narrowing his eyes, he hissed, "Remember, if you do, I will be there to right your path." He turned abruptly around and ran down the mountain, trusting his massive snowshoe paws to safely get him down.

Chapter 10

Lynx traveled on, observing the small hills and valleys of this new land. There were trees and shrubs, and animals that he had never seen before. Like those enormous ground squirrels with the spikey tails. They were almost as large as Clarence, which could be scary. Hearing movement in the distance made him pause and move his ears around to hear better. Closing his eyes, he hoped to get a visual of what was coming his way.

"You're cute," he heard a female voice say, giggling. Lynx's eyes flew open to see a werecat standing on her back legs, half in human form and half in her feline form. Her triangular furry face, front legs and upper torso were orange with black spots, and her lower half was human. Her front paws were paws but she would shift them into hands when needed. She wore a purple cotton baggy wrap-around that Lynx couldn't decide if it were pants or a skirt. She also had a tail, with a little tassel on the end of it. She appeared odd to him. But she was attractive – a little drink of water- he remembered hearing Mark, Xander's father, describing Erin that way. The female werecat tilted her head down, fluttering her eyelids. "I haven't seen you around here before. Where are you from?"

"Not from here," Lynx said slowly. "Um, I guess you could say I'm new here." He felt his face flush. "Um, can you tell me where the village is?"

"The Ohanaian's village?" she asked. Lynx nodded. "You don't want to go there, fella. That's not a place for us werecats. But hey, you don't look like a true werecat. What're you hiding?"

"What am I hiding?" Lynx replayed the words as soon as he spoke them and they sounded too harsh, angry. "I'm not hiding anything. Why would you think that?"

"Because you aren't in your true form."

"True form? Well, you aren't either! Who are you to judge me?" Lynx bellowed.

"I'm Lyraca. I'm the one who is chosen to represent us to the Ohanaians when they hold council meetings that concern all those who live on Ohana. The only beings who aren't invited to the table are the bears because they won't live by the Ohanaian's laws. We don't always, either. But there is a massive problem with Ohanaian's little ones running amuck, harassing our cubs. Years ago, one of the cubs from our nest vanished in a blazing fire. Someone said a bear cub set the wagon on fire and another said it was the Ohanaian's cubs that were chasing the poor frightened cub. The adult Ohanaian's said the parents of the werecub should have been more watchful."

Lynx gulped. "But someone saved that werecub . . . right?"

"I'm not sure. No one knows because then something strange happened. It was an odd day with many off-worlders coming through the portals that few people know about." Lyraca confessed. Her yellow eyes became slits as she scanned Lynx closer. Her whiskers twitched. Opening her eyes wide, "You have deep wounds. And part of you is closed off. You aren't sleeping well because something is plaguing you. Come, follow me. I will take you to Soul Healer."

"Soul Healer?" Lynx said.

"He is the one who heals those of us that suffer traumas and injuries. I sense you have that trauma. That someone bewitched you. What's your name?" Lyraca started out and Lynx followed her.

"Lynx. But I doubt that was my original name. I remember being a runt . . ."

"It was a runt that vanished about four years ago. Others say it perished in a fire. Soul Healer said otherwise."

Birds sang as they went, but one stood out with an ear-splitting tune that made Lynx want to cover his ears. "What's wrong with that one bird that's answering the first?"

"Nothing. When it was a chick, it disobeyed one of the bear gods so the bear god punished it, almost crushing its throat. Soul Healer managed to save the bird's life but couldn't restore his singing box. Others have accepted him, and his mate is dedicated to him. He is also a good provider, sharing all the caregiving with his mate."

"Bear gods?" Lynx said, "There's bears here who rule the forest?"

"Yes, but they don't mess with us. We don't honor or worship them. Other of the animals do. Some bring them their kills and willingly bow down so the bears won't kill their young or wipe out their whole family units." Lyraca explained.

As they walked, Lyraca shifted to her full werecat form, a sleek, orange and black spotted feline shape with pointed fangs and a whip like tail.

Turning around, Lynx felt both repulsed by the half human form and attracted to her werecat form.

Though, something familiar struck him. His mind showed him a memory of his mom. But Lyraca couldn't be related to him. Shaking his head, he asked.

"Do the Ohanaians recognize the bears as gods?"

"No. They respect the bears, not because they're gods – but because they're powerful and have killed many of them on hunts. There is a story of a young bear that learned to make fire. He disappeared at the same time as the werecub runt. That bear cub was close to adulthood, I think, so he was older than the werecat. According to Soul Healer, the bear went to another world that was different than were the werecub went to."

The sky gradually changed from a blue to slightly orange tinge with yellow streaks. Lynx wondered if the sky changed color because his emotions were causing it, like in Curá.

"It's late in the afternoon, Lynx. The daylight will be vanishing soon, and it will be time for our nightly hunt. But first, let's go to the werecat village." Lyraca turned down a winding meadow with few trees and filled with a mixture of soft and stiff grasses. Some of them looked like the type of grass the Murdocs would be using to weave rugs, and the roofs of their huts. But he expected swamps. Taking a deep breath, Lynx inhaled the fragrant scents of the different types of flowers and grasses, and then something buzzed around him and ended up going up his nose. He sneezed violently, spraying Lyraca with spittle.

"Eww! Gross." She shook herself off, her spine wrinkling up. Then she laughed. "You got to be careful of those tiny tube flies. They love checking out new critters who come enter the village."

"Tube flies?" Lynx asked.

"Yes, tube flies. They live in the tube gardens. The Ohanaians and others gather the tube when they dry out so they can weave rugs, wall hangings and some even dye them to create the symbol of their creator being," Lyraca shrugged. "Frankly, I don't get it. But they feel a connection to all nature through honoring it."

"Can you explain what they worship?" Lynx ran to catch up to her. She shook her head.

"Not really. Soul Healer probably can. Right now, we need to get you some food and find out who you are and where you came from."

Lynx's stomach rumbled.

There were about six werecubs playing outside the cave as they approached. Lynx heard something in a nearby tree, the limbs rattled, causing him to jump and look up.

"Yaller, get out that tree!" Lyraca yelled out. "Mammy won't like you being up there."

"Naw, Lyraca. Mammy said I could be up here. I asked. I know I can climb, what are claws for if I can't get up and down?" Yaller yelled back. He slowly made his way to the strongest branch of the tree. "Besides, this tree speaks to me."

"Trees don't talk, silly!" Lyraca replied.

"This is one does! You just gotta know how to talk with it." The little cub yawned, stretching out. "I'm going to take a nap, like the Ohanaian cubs do." He yawned again.

Lynx followed Lyraca in, who was shaking her head and clicking her tongue.

"Why don't you want him in the tree?" Lynx asked.

"He has quite the imagination. Says there are beasts that swing from limb to limb, jumping from one tree branch and landing in a nearby tree. He aspires to be like that. But has broken his legs many times in his short life. He doesn't listen."

"He's a runt, isn't he?" Lynx was amazed.

"No. Most runts don't survive here. Especially the ones that don't conform to the were laws."

"Like what?"

"Like not speaking right away. Refusing to shapeshift between two to six months or won't kneel to an older sibling. Most runts abide by the laws – except those who are born with a substandard development. When that happens, sometimes we must give them the fire test. See if they can survive walking through a fire to become the demon cat the Ohanaians are afraid of. Others refuse. If a runt makes it to a village before the fire test, then there is more trouble and they were branded a demon by them which makes it worse. Most runts aren't willing to learn. They're stubborn, and often get blackballed unless an older brother chases them out before the fire test."

Lynx remembered his dream, trembling, his face went pale.

"What's wrong? You look like someone walked across your grave," another voice spoke up. Lynx gulped, turning his gaze to an older werecat, who was bright purple with silly pink stripes.

"Nothing. Just remembered a nightmare," Lynx said in a low voice. The other one laughed.

"Nightmares, eh? You must be a weakling. Only cubs have nightmares. We give the nightmares," the large purple werecat jutted out his chin. "I'm Torrid." He held out his right paw, Lynx thought they were supposed to shake it. But realized this new werecat didn't have thumbs, like he had. Lynx smiled and held out his paw.

Torrid lightly tapped the back of Lynx's paw with the back of his extended paw then tapped the front, so they tapped pads.

"I'm Lynx."

"You aren't a demon, are you? You never went through a fire --- you have to be initiated."

Lynx gulped, remembering the dream cub bursting into flames. "I'm no demon, but others have called me one."

"Look! He has opposable toes like the Ohanaians!" Yaller shouted, pointing at Lynx's extra toes. "He's been altered without shifting! How did that happen?" Lynx jumped, not hearing Yaller come inside.

"I can't tell you. But that's why I was called a demon – they were created. . ."

"If they were, then they can be uncreated. That is the werecat way," an old voice stated, hobbling in.

Lynx's head swam, a rush of warm air, like Erin opened the oven door to take out a roast for dinner at the same time he was strolling through the house to head upstairs to the boys' room. The cave weaved in and out. The voices around him started yelling directions to catch him, but it sounded like they were speaking from above while he was underwater. Everything went dark.

The air blew cold. A voice in the distance called him, but the name uttered wasn't the one he knew. Lynx peered down at his body. This felt safe. But it was wrong to be floating above his body. A vague feeling like he'd done this before.

"Come, Beelzebub. Come follow me. I'll show where you need to be," the voice stated.

"I'm not Beelzebub. I'm Lynx," he said, floating out the door. The air blew around him, but no body showed itself. "Where are you? Who are you?"

"It matters not who I am. At one time, I was called Claude. But don't call me that now. I prefer to be unseen and I won't recognize you nor you me. After my initiation my name was changed. It's my fault you got lost."

"What happened?" Lynx said. "Were you in the room that I just left?"

"Yes. Part of me is still in that room. Follow me. Mud is never clear until all the filth is washed away. We choose our path. But you haven't chosen all of yours. It was derailed and I'm the one who caused it."

"Can you please reveal yourself so I can see where we are heading?" Lynx asked, scanning the sky and the forest as they flew.

"Spirit seldom reveals us a physical form. Soul Healer taught me how to stay invisible when I need to be. My gift is to be in two places at once. When it is time, you will know who I am in the were nest."

As they soared on, Lynx scanned the forest floor and spotted Manx running like his tail was ablaze.

Something wasn't right. Lynx knew that Artaois had to be in this world, too, and Manx was there to protect him, while teaching Artaois a lesson. Though, Lynx didn't know how he knew. He just knew it. Yet he knew Manx hated him.

"You know that strange cat down there, Beelzebub?" Claude asked.

"Yes. He is an apprentice to someone who travels to other worlds. Manx is being trained to work with the animals, I'm guessing. There is a bear who is telling me to be afraid of the humans . . ."

"Ohanaians? Why?" Claude was surprised.

"Not sure. Said they caused me pain before. I can't remember much of my cub years."

"They've been blocked. Soul Healer will show you. Now, I will tell you something else. Land on this rock."

Lynx did. As he did, he noticed the air shimmering. "Claude, is that you?"

"Yes, it is. Remember when we were cubs? I was your older brother. I called you runt. I bit off part of your ear and knocked you against the wall of the nest. Mamma and Dadpa punished me by telling me to help nurse you back to health. But no one knew what happened."

"You lost me. What happened?" Lynx said. "I have a vague recollection . . ."

"I resented having to care for you, a runt. You ruined my stride and demanded food when there wasn't any. Somehow, Mamma was always able to feed you. One day, I chased you out of the nest. I chased you and the last thing I remember was a bear cub, almost a grown

bear, chasing after you. You were too young to know not to play with bears or understand how they can play with a werecat's mind. I said I didn't care. But I regret . . ."

Something pulled at Lynx's spirit. It didn't feel right. "Not Beelzebub. No, that wasn't me. Whatever happened, you aren't Claude. How can you know? There wasn't a bear – and it couldn't have been me. Village, I need to find the village. Gotta go back to my body. . ."

"Wait. You are Beelzebub. I know you are. I see your true form. You have part of your ear missing when I bit it a week or two after I knocked you out. . ."

"No, no no! I refuse to believe. Lyraca told me about the runt that vanished. A bear. Now you are saying it was me? Can't be me!" Lynx flew back to his body.

Lynx saw the group gathered around his body. There was a fire in the center, so they had moved his body towards it to keep it warm. But his image shimmered, going from his Maine Coon body to how he appeared on Curá, as a tabby cat with an attitude to an orange and black striped cat with a lean body and a crooked tail, with half his right ear missing and scars on his right side showing wrinkled skin. Lynx was repulsed, but the image shifted back to the Maine Coon. His heart exploded with love and acceptance for it, but then he noticed the older werecat, with the greying fur on top of his head and face, crooked whiskers, that looked up and waved a front paw toward him.

"It's time you come back to your shell so we can talk," the older werecat said. Lynx obeyed.

Opening his eyes, he yawned. "What happened?" he said and started to sit up. An Ohanaian boy came in with a cup of steaming brew. Kneeling, he offered it to Lynx.

"This is Manheim. He was sent here a year ago to tend to us, and train with me before he goes on to work with his people. I'm Soul Healer," the older werecat said. "Drink this brew slowly. We make it for all who have lost their way. The All That Is speaks loud to you, Lynx. But you don't listen. You've lost your way and have allowed others to taint your shapeshifting. You've forgotten . . ."

"He hasn't been taught. He vanished before he could be shown," said the one with the purple fur and pink stripes. Lynx remembered his name was Torrid. Yeah . . . but then he felt woozy again. Shaking his head, to dispel the cobwebs, he remembered.

"I asked a question – what happened?"

"Well, no one knocked you into a wall this time, runt!" Torrid snapped. Lynx's jaw flew open.

"Torrid, that's enough! You're too big to be sent to your room and this is no runt," Soul Healer admonished. "Something jilted you – shock. Do you know where you are?"

Lynx shook his head. Lyraca . . . he looked around the room and saw her sitting in the corner rocking a young werecub. "Lyraca spoke of Ohanaians, like you did. But I don't know the name of this world."

"This is Ohana. The Land. You're with your kind. You need to remember who you are and we need to release that block. But first, you must rest." Soul Healer stood up, using a staff with the Albagoth symbol so he could steady himself on his back legs. Lynx noticed Soul Healer had shifted his paw so it could grasp the staff. Soul Healer glanced down.

"You have friends who are looking for you. And you want to visit the Ohanaian's village, correct?"

Lynx nodded. "When we first got to this world, my inner voice said to go the village. But I don't understand why. I'm looking for answers and a solution to my nightmares. And," his voice trailed, wondering if he said it.

"Go on."

"That Bear warned me to stay away . . . from . . . humans . . ." Lynx muttered. Then thought it sounded silly to say that.

Soul Healer laughed. "He won't hurt you. I saw images of that bear. He is under a cloud, too. His brain has been rattled. Get some rest. I will send Torrid and others to look for your friends, a domestic short cat, a griffin and a river rodent, am I correct?"

"Yes," Lynx suddenly felt like he was a helpless cub.

"Drink your brew. It has herbs that will assist you to sleep and rest. As we work with you, we will help you to remember what happened the day you vanished."

"You know me?" Lynx said.

"Of course. We see your true form, and you will learn what happened. Tomorrow go into the town. Lyraca will go with you."

A light breeze rustled the nearby dry weeds, tall, hollow tube plants, flowers and small trees, ruffling Artaois' fur as he wandered through the meadows in the heavy darkness looking for a place to build a fire to start his new assault on Lynx. He had no idea of where that stupid werecat could be. This world was strange, yet familiar and he couldn't remember.

After he found a place that had the remnants of a fire where humans or, *what did Annila call them? Ohanaians? Had built one. Perhaps I could use it and start that fire again.* Artaois sat down, remembering the female that claimed to be his sister said he used to create fire by rubbing his paws together. Starting slowly, he decided to see what would happen. Then the thought popped into his mind – he wasn't familiar with any of the plant life here. Could he find feline loco weed? Could he find any of the other plants that would cause his enchantments to work? Sighing heavily, Artaois stood to his full height on his back legs and paced around. As he scanned the landscape, Artaois knew he was a god of this world, too. If this was his birth world, then maybe someone ought to help him out.

Hearing a night bird cawing and hooting nearby, the bear closed his eyes to pinpoint where it was coming from, hoping it was like that owl back home.

Home? Wasn't this supposed to be his true home? But it all felt wrong and odd. But it should feel wrong.

"You want to ask a question. You're looking to bewitch someone?" A small voice asked.

Artaois looked down, seeing a tiny creature about the size of a mouse, but had the face and head of horse, but so small he would have stepped on it.

"What do you know of enchantments?" Artaois roared. "You're a puny thing and very ugly."

"What I lack in beauty I make up in know-how," said the animal.

"And how about, what do you know?" Artaois giggled at his word choice. The animal growled and spat.

"I know you aren't a god. I know you're a fool who thinks you can outsmart a werecat who has magic he doesn't realize he has access to. Once he does, he will show you to be the fool that you have always been."

"How dare you!" roared the bear.

"Yes, I dare. I also know more about spells and enchantments than you have on your tiny toe. But I will tell you where you can find the locoweed that drives the werecats crazy. Be forewarned, however. It is against Ohana law to use it to bewitch werecats and other animals. It is especially forbidden to use it if you are a bear believing your godhood is ordained while denying the All That Is, is central to all living beings," the odd creature said.

"Why would you share that knowledge with me?"

"I share it because it is in my nature to assist another to indulge in their foolish pride and desire to harm another when it is bound to backfire. Remember, that what you send out to the universe will come back to you ten-fold."

Artaois threw back his head and laughed deeply and long. Suddenly, the little creature growled, then a spark of brilliant light caused Artois to close his eyes. When he opened them, the creature had grown to the size of pony. It had a horse head and the body of a rat, with a long whip tail.

"What are you?" Artaois trembled.

"I'm a Raworse. I help those who are bent on destroying themselves. Just like you."

"What?" Artaois couldn't believe his ears. "I won't destroy myself! I am a god! In a long line of gods before me!"

"Gods are immortal, Artaois. If you are so godly, then why were you born? And why have your ancestors died? Wake up and smell the Morning Beans."

Artaois didn't know what to say.

"Magic is yours if you believe. But sometimes you just must be you. Fire in your heart can create the fire of innocence. Or it can grow out of hand and devour all you care about. You, Artaois, only care about yourself. And you rule others out of fear. You have no joy. No love."

"I heard I made fire once . . ."

"Innocence, my dear bear god. Must remember. Two stones and dry weeds," the Raworse said.

Artaois knitted his brows together, thinking and not liking what he was hearing. "Why would I have to use two stones and dry weeds to make fire? When all I have to do is clap my paws." The bear demonstrated, causing the Raworse to back up in fright.

"Now, you are going to show me where to find the locoweed."

"Sure. It's over under the rocks and near the pond that eventually flows to the river. Just don't disturb the river mammals." The Raworse smiled, his eyes twinkling in the moonlight. "It isn't far from here."

Artaois turned to his left, hearing the pond rippling in the distance. When he turned back, the strange creature was gone. Artaois lumbered in that direction and gathered all he could find, hoping he didn't have to dry it out. He was afraid he had lost too much time as it was. He was afraid that the effects of his last enchantment were wearing off Lynx and the werecat would be less able to be influenced to live the nightmare of his cubhood.

Once he had gathered all the dry tree limbs and enough of the locoweed, Artaois sat down, stretching out his back so he could concentrate on creating the flames he needed. Indeed, he wondered how he started the fires under his large cauldron back home. He did it without thinking about it. Inhaling deeply and letting it out slowly, he summoned fire, stretching out his paws, pads down. He could feel them heating up. Opening his eyes, he smiled as he saw flames shooting out from the center pad of both front paws, starting the wood and locoweeds ablaze.

"I am the most powerful god alive!" Artaois shouted. "I can do all things through my own strength!" He started chanting, "Remember, Lynx. Remember the frightened cub you were. Running from your nest. Running to the village. Seeing the Ohanaians terrified of you . . . See the anger and hatred they had – they chased you . . . See the fire . . ."

"Grow fire – blaze fiercely—" Artaois danced around the inferno, lulling himself into a hypnotic state, living what he envisioned through his message. Fear – terror. Delighting in the pain he wanted Lynx to experience. "I will destroy you . . ." feeling his spiritual body rising above the physical one, Artaois' consciousness soared to where Lynx was laying down to sleep.

Lynx drank the brew that the Ohanaian boy gave him. It tasted like cinnamon bark mixed with roses petals, lavender and smooth chamomile. His eyes shut involuntarily, which annoyed him because there were still others in the nest milling around, talking in soft tones, and he wanted to hear what they were saying. *There had to be something in this besides those herbs. I think that the one they called Soul Healer is bewitching me . . .*

"Hush, just sleep," Lyraca said in her melodic voice as if she was talking to a stubborn werecub refusing to sleep. "You've had a long day. It's time to rest."

Lynx's eyes closed again. Abruptly, he felt his spirit yanked out of his body and then slammed back in, startling him with a yip, and his eyes flew open and the others glared at him. The adults shushed everyone, and ushered them out of the room. Soul Healer and his apprentice put the fire out. His eyes closed again.

A pungent aroma drifted into the cave; an unconscious Lynx took a deep breath, slowly exhaled, smacking his lips. He stretched his body out as he laid down, going deeper into sleep. Another wave of odor mixed with low muttering chants which only came to his ears, made them twitch as the message went into his slumber. Breathing slower, he rolled over.

Albagoth, you often assist Xander, Geoffrey and Milo. Lynx exhaled, as his spirt rose again from the sleeping body. What am I supposed to know? How am I to overcome this or face this? I'm confused and unsure of myself.

Lynx saw himself running through rocky terrain. Not far behind was a pack of humans, but they wore loose fitting shirts that tucked under their legs and knee length trousers. Some carried spears, others held torches and pitchforks. They yelled and screamed. The wind spun around the werecat as he dodged a steep incline with a tree not too far off. One giant leap, and he landed up in the fork between the trunk and sturdiest of the limbs before it branched out. But the winds were too strong, and they threw him out, spinning him around, tail first. The villagers shouted at him.

"You can't escape us! We'll get you demon! You're more than evil. Bewitched. You are horrible – worse than any werecat! Listen to us!"

"Reveal who is directing you," the werecat demanded. "Wind put me down! Obey me!"

Abruptly Lynx fell, landing among a circle of bears holding each other's paws while they chanted and swayed around a fire. As he circled, he could see each of the faces – they all looked like Artaois, except one with a scar which stretched across his left eye, which reminded him of a pirate Xander had once shown him the picture of. Only a pirate in a bear costume that looked too real. He realized they were all Artaois – the chanting was clear before the winds increased, whipping him around so fast the faces became a blur.

"You are not who you think you are. Gods are to be feared. Ohanaians are to be feared. Remember the torture. Remember the flames as they singed your fur, kissing the skin and leaving their marks."

Lynx's fur began to curl as the flames touched him; panic spread through his nervous system. His legs moved to run away. His heart pounded in chest. He struggled to scream but his throat closed . . . A solid stone wall rose up blocking the flames from hurting him further.

The scene shifted to Lynx as a werecub running with oversized paws away from Ohanaian youths as they taunted him, crying out for the demon cat to stop. Suddenly, a bear engulfed in flames that didn't devour him appeared, "No one tells you what to do. But I will tell you! You vile werecat! Playing with Ohanaians! They are your destruction! I am your law!"

Lynx panted, out of breath and not knowing who the greater threat was. The bear or the youths. A large hole opened under himself and the bear and he felt helpless, falling through. Lynx woke up in a sweat, paws flaring and yelling.

Chapter 11

A loud snap jarred Artaois out of his stupor. The sky above him spun at a breakneck speed, causing him to wonder what happened. Gradually, it slowed down, as he replayed the visions and realized the connection to Lynx had been broken. *But what happened to break it? And how can I reestablish it?*

Sitting up was a feat, because it caused him to feel dizzier and more nauseous. He slowly lowered himself back down and rolled on his sides, his mind swimming, he could still feel his spirit hovering over his body, but it felt like something else was there, too.

"Who's that?" Artaois addressed the entity, narrowing his eyes to see.

"I'm the one known in this world as the All That Is," a mysterious voice boomed.

"My family and tribe are the only gods of this world," Artaois replied. "You don't matter."

"I created all worlds and all living people, animals, minerals, plants and water on each of them. That means, I created you bears, too," All That Is replied.

Artaois laughed.

"All of my people and animals matter to me. Even you, Artaois."

Artaois shook his head as he laughed. "You're misguided. If you were so awesome and caring, I'd be able to see you. What really is a werecat to you?"

"They are special to me because they are able to shift from one body to the next. And they are unique to this world. Except one small werecat. He is dearer to me because he has explored other worlds. And he is the one you are terrorizing. Leave him alone, or you will be answering to me. I will show you my true form – I am awesome and wonderfully made."

Artaois threw back and his head and laughed out loud. "You sound like those stupid humans! I've heard their sermons where they praise their imaginary creator. How stupid can they be? We bears are the only gods to be feared. We are awesome and wonderfully made. We don't bow down to anyone or any deity because we are above that!"

The ground shook and twisted so violently, the grizzly thought he was in a joy ride he heard described by a former circus bear who escaped to go back to the wild, jarring him in such a way that his spirit slammed back into his body. As it spun, he heard the words echo throughout, "Leave Lynx alone! Stop your conjuring and torture! Continue it, and you will find out who the real demon is!"

The entity left at the same time the land stopped shaking, leaving a vacuum which sucked Artaois' breath, thoughts and emotion out of him.

The early morning light embraced Lynx through a natural opening in the cave. Lynx slowly opened his eyes. His head felt like a ton of bricks was tied to it and his body and limbs ached as if he had been running all night. Muffled voices stirred him to get up; he heard soft paw steps rushing to his side.

"Careful, take it slow," Lyraca's gentle voice urged him. "Soul Healer's tea will leave you with a bit of a hangover."

"You're still having nightmares, despite what I prepared you," Soul Healer added. "Whoever is bewitching you is intent on making sure you stay scared and exhausted."

Lynx nodded, as the thoughts and images from his dreams flooded his vision. Scrunching his eyes to shut them out, "Not exhausted – only sore. I feel like I hit a wall and slid down hitting the ground hard. There's no cushions."

"It's that bear I'm in charge of," said a new voice.

"Manx?" Lynx sat up so fast he almost fainted. "What're you doing here? How did you find me?"

"Albagoth sent Sage Tomás and me to your world to check on Artaois. I was assigned to guide and teach him. He's one stubborn bear," Manx replied. "My mission is two-fold. You are the second part. To protect you and get you to face your true self."

"My true self?" Lynx said. "I am who I really am. I'm not hiding anything!"

Manx abruptly stood and got in the werecat's face. "Really? Then shift into your original body."

Lynx backed up, cringing. "No! I can't! I -I-I . . ."

"Can't? Or won't?" Manx demanded. "I never liked you because you're hiding something, Lynx! You don't know who you really are! You are what others tell you to be! Alchemist Tarrier tells you to be a tame pussy cat, ignoring your natural werecat instincts! You obediently believe him! The Reflection Pond shows you a Maine Coon cat from the World of Nampa, so totally out of place for Curá, and you happily adopt it. Why can't you just face who you were born to be?"

"Because Tarrier said it would scare the Kentians and said my body had scars that no one needed to see. I can't remember my birth shape. I'm not a demon, Manx. I –I-I," Lynx hung his head.

"Scared?" Lyraca filled in.

"It hurts, Manx. My head. My heart. Whenever the nightmares come, I can see glimpses of my early years – but I can't remember it all." Lynx took a deep breath and let it out.

Soul Healer cleared his throat, getting the attention of the others; they looked at him. "Lynx, you asked how Manx found you. Our scouts found him collapsed near the cave, exhausted, dehydrated and half-starved. They brought him back here, before realizing he wasn't a werecat at all. We still welcomed him because I noticed All That Is walks with him. He whispered to me that you're in dire trouble and we need to help him."

"How long have you been out there?" Lynx asked.

"I don't have a sense of how many days have gone by. Artaois sent me away a while ago, and I didn't know how to find the werecat cave. I ran down the mountain and have been out in the desert for a while, not finding food nor water. I paused, to get my bearings closer to here, going by inner directions, more than certainty. I passed out. Then the scouts found me and dragged me here. Soul Healer gave me some herbal tea and food to revive me."

"I see," Lynx said slowly. He thought of Geoffrey, Clarence and Wayohm. "What about my friends that I came here with? Were the scouts able to find them?"

"Yes, they are resting in the nursey with the werecubs," Lyraca answered. "We will get you and Manx some food. You and I have a journey to the

Ohanaian village to begin some of your journey to piece together your past."

"Not so fast," Soul Healer directed. The old werecat shaman stood up and came over to them, "Lynx and I need to have a private consultation before you two take off. Manx, there is food in the back. Lyraca, please go and have my other apprentice bring Lynx and me some of the meal."

"Yes, Soul Healer," she bowed and left.

Lynx's heart thudded in his chest as he watched her retreating hips sway –did she always look like this? Human from the waist down, with a perfect hourglass figure that most females back home would kill for and the top half remained a furry, orange and lavender striped werecat. Though she had human arms and hands. Her bright purple whiskers twitched as she glanced over her shoulder, flashing him a mischievous smile as her orange eyes sparkled. She turned around, and he noticed her fluffy lavender and pink striped tail swaying back and forth from the human buttocks in a hypnotizing manner. He realized Lyraca kept changing her colors, and each time, she was more breathtaking. Then it occurred to him that his jaw was open, and he had stopped breathing. Closing his mouth to stop the drool, he felt the heat rush to his cheeks, and quelled the urge to chase her.

"Be careful with that one, Lynx. As most werecats here, she isn't what she appears to be. She loves to play with male's emotions like we would play with our prey before we pounce for the kill," Soul Healer cautioned.

Lynx blinked and looked down at the ground. The Ohanaian helper came in with two plates of what looked like cooked meat, tubers and vegetables. The smell reminded him of Erin's cooking. The Ohanaian put the plate down.

"What's your name?" Lynx asked him. The boy's eyes grew to two round black discs.

"I don't have a name yet. I'm learning to be a healer so I can go back to my village. But Soul Healer sometimes needs one Ohanaian to assist him with the chores and care of the tribe here."

"Are you a slave?" Lynx asked. He glanced away, not sure if he should have said that.

Soul Healer chuckled. The boy looked at him. "Go ahead and answer. I don't hold your tongue, boy."

"No, I'm not. I have a gift of seeing things before they happen. I knew which herbs to harvest without being taught. My mom knew our village healer didn't have the knowledge to help me so I was sent here. I'm an equal as equal as a cub can be to their elders. I am one of the werecats – except I can't shift into animal form." The boy looked away.

"You're hiding something," Lynx said, narrowing his eyes.

"Yes, he is. It is rumored that his mom had mated with a werecat when he was in human form. It wasn't her choice, and the boy has werecat blood running through his veins. If that is true, he would be able to shift. We are monitoring him for now to see what happens when he reaches his eighth year. Humans mature at a slower rate than we do. A werecub can usually shift by their first year. Except Torrid and Claude. They shifted much earlier because of their dominance to the others of his nest mates born at the same time." The old werecat took the plate and nodded to his apprentice. "Thank you. You may leave. We will begin lessons in a moment. Assist with cleaning the dishes and set out what needs to be taught."

"Yes, Healer," the boy bowed, turned and left.

Lynx narrowed his eyes, his heart grieving for the boy's mom being raped. He wondered if the Ohanaians would have held the rapist accountable or what happened. Surely there would have been torches and gangs chasing the rapist for what he did. Then another thought came to him: there might be more to that story, too. Sighing, he realized it was best he didn't know all the details since he was new to this society.

They ate in silence. Lynx studied the elder werecat's face, wishing he had Xander's gift for seeing inside another's mind. A small voice reminded him that he knew the Ohanaian boy was hiding something. But it puzzled him. Shaking his head, he wondered what it was. The whole mess here was curious. Cocking his head to one side, he brought his ears forward.

Lynx glanced around the cave, noticing every indent and bulge. Memories of being a werecub exploring the alcoves and passageways fascinated him, causing him to wonder if they were true memories or just him imagining. Then a bug came into view followed by an insect that looked like a spider. The spider paused, lifted a front leg and waved at him, causing Lynx to do a double take. When he looked again, the spider had captured the smaller bug and held it fast in its two front legs and was busy eating it. *Yum*, Lynx thought sarcastically. His mind switched back to the present.

"You wanted to speak with me alone. Why?"

Soul Healer put the plate down. "We werecats are a curious breed. We can eat like humans, as you learned to call them. You've been to other worlds, Lynx – your formative years were not on Ohana. But this is your birth world. Someone has put a block on your memory. A curse so you no longer remember all of us. Fire started unlocking this curse. What do you remember?"

"Curse?" the words startled him. Shaking his head, he thought of Tarrier. "Tarrier wouldn't curse me. He said he removed the hurtful time as he healed my wounds. He didn't want me to carry the inner scares of what others did to me. Nor did he want me to live in a body that reminded me and others what happened. He said if I ever shifted into my body with the scars, others would recoil in fear and call me demon cat . . ."

"It would have hurt his business," Soul Healer replied. "Let's be honest. It was for his benefit. Not yours. He did you no favors, Lynx. You need to remember. Tell me what your nightmares are. Tell me about this bear that Manx is supposed to be guiding and teaching."

Lynx put his plate down and cleared his throat; the scenes from his first nightmares played in his mind. Closing his eyes tight, he willed them to stop. He sighed.

"I dreamed – or relived- part of my cub years. I was about a month or two old. My older brother, Claude, wanted me to leave the nest. He called me runt and I couldn't speak. He called me inferior. Said no one loved me and Mamma and Dadpa didn't want me, either. He knocked me against the wall, rendering me unconscious. My spirit rose out of my body and went to a bear family that had killed two Ohanaian men and they were feasting on the meat. The youngest looked up and pointed to me, said I was a dead werecat. He wanted to send my spirit to the afterlife. His papa back pawed him, saying werecats didn't have souls. Therefore, there was no afterlife for me. My soul was pulled back to my body as someone was dragging me to a fire and I heard an older werecat, maybe you? Chanting over me and trying to wake me up. My Mamma was weeping over me."

Soul Healer nodded. "Yes, that all happened. What else do you remember?"

Lynx thought back over the last few days. Shaking his head- flashes of flames came to mind- causing him to flinch and scoot back as if it was real. "Flames!"

"What?" The elder werecat, moved closer to his patient. "Flames?"

"Yes." Lynx flinched again. "Uh – Tarrier said he found me under a burning wagon. He managed to pull me out. He didn't say he found me on another world. To my knowledge, he hasn't been off Curá. If I was from here, then it would be sensible for there to be other werecats there. But I was the only one. I never thought about it being odd, before. Until now." A lump rose to Lynx's throat, he felt tears rising. "I'm not supposed to have tear ducts . . ."

"All werecats have tear ducts," Soul Healer said. "Your friend, Tarrier, lied to you."

"Lied? But he helped me! He gave me thumbs!" Lynx held up his front paws.

Soul Healer laughed. "No, he knew how to trigger your ability to shift individual parts of your body and paws to create the thumbs. He just wanted you to believe he gave them to you using his alchemical skills."

"But he was a friend and my caregiver!"

"Maybe so – but he didn't have your best interest at heart. He was afraid of what his customers would say. . ."

"How do you know what he was afraid of? Or what he did for a living!" Lynx fired at him. "What makes you such an expert on a man who you never met?" Lynx stood on his back legs and lunged at the old healer.

Soul Healer held up his staff he used to assist him to walk on his hind legs, sending Lynx back towards the wall. Lynx felt the cave spinning around, briefly, but a single word uttered by the healer ceased it.

"What if I tell you I knew Tarrier before he went back to the world that became his home? He came here with another traveler. They visited the cave because he was being trained to be a Spiritual guide who traveled to other worlds. Most of us back then enjoyed our appearance. We go through the fire of initiation to choose who we are to become, demon or not. Once we embrace who and what we are, we can shift, if we want to. Those who refuse to go through the fire are not kept in the tribe. They are sent out. Those that choose to become demon werecats are also excommunicated."

"So, I didn't hide under a wagon to avoid kids who were taunting me? And they didn't set me on fire?" Lynx asked.

"There was a bear that could call fire down and it came through his paws. He had an unusual attraction to you. Wherever you went, he wasn't far behind. On

the day Tarrier took you, the bear followed, calling
for you to run away. Saying you were in trouble. It
was dangerous . . . The bear managed to wrestle you
out of Tarrier's arms. An inferno came down . . .
sending you up in flames. You weren't initiated – if
you were, the fire wouldn't have hurt you. But Tarrier
and his master teacher, Sage Tomás, called down
rains to put the fire out and then the master teacher
opened a portal, sending the bear cub away after
wiping his memory. Only, he didn't forget you. He
found you. Somehow . . ."

"Sage Tomás accidentally linked you and Artaois
together. So, when you came to the World of Nampa,
Artaois knew you were there before he even saw you.
This is where I come in," Manx said.

Manx's footsteps were so soft, they hadn't heard him
come into the room.

Chapter 12

Lynx and Lyraca walked towards the Ohanaian village. It was a sunny day and a light breeze blew her facial and ear tufts, which enflamed his body. Lynx longed to sniff her scent and breathe deeply of all her being, becoming one with her until they both yowled with pleasure. He did his best not to show it. *I'm not her kind, or type,* he told himself.

"Why do we need to go into town again?" Lynx asked wondering if they could turn around or do something else. It didn't feel right to go into town for some reason.

Birds above them called to each other as they played aerial tag. He wanted to walk on four feet, but Lyraca convinced him to walk on his hind legs, like he did in Wayla.

Lyraca smiled, shaking her head, "You have a short memory, Runt."

"I do?" he uttered, half-joking. He did remember his inner voice, maybe it was Albagoth, saying to go to the town to piece together what happened. But now, he wasn't so sure this was the right thing to do.

"Yes, you do. You said yesterday that a voice inside yourself said to go to the town. Soul Healer asked me to accompany you because I'm the ambassador to their council. They will talk with me."

"Why you?"

"Because I am comfortable shifting into Ohanaian form. Few Ohanaians will accept a werecat in their animal form. We could become whatever we need to be. Or what we think will express who our soul is. Claude is a rebel and outcast. He chooses bright, warning, colors for his fur to show his disregard for authority. His offspring will not share his company for long. No one will mate with him willingly."

Lynx shrugged. "But how come you're comfortable as a human? I mean, I guess Ohanaians are human?"

"I suppose they are," she glanced at him from her peripheral vision. "We never stopped to consider it since it is rare for us to have visitors from other worlds that All That Is created." Lyraca said. The shrubs around them rustled at the same time they heard thundering feet as if there was a stampede of horses. They turned to see a tribe of massive animals that reminded Lynx of elk running their way. On their heels were a group of bears, herding them into a corner. Lyraca pushed Lynx out of the way toward a large boulder.

"What's wrong?" Lynx shouted as they fell behind the large mound of rock. One of the bears paused to sniff the air as the others continued their chase. Lyraca landed on top of him and he smiled suggestively. "You just want to take advantage of a guy once he's down, right?" he wiggled his ears and twitched his whiskers. She slugged him.

"Look you! Those bears are dangerous critters! They're all deluded, believing they are the gods of the animal world and they want nothing to do with Ohanaians! Any animal that ignores them and follows the true creator gets run over or banished. They believe all werecats are bad. I want to keep you safe because you weren't raised here!"

"No! I wasn't. But I can take care of myself!"

"No, you can't! Bears believe they're entitled to tell others what to do and to rule everyone! They either run from us or attack us werecats because we don't accept their rules! And especially you, because you have a bear who is hot on your tail!" Lyraca hissed, her fur stood out, making her look ten times larger – Lynx scooted back away from her. They heard something scampering up the boulder toward them. "Now! Hush!" she lowered her voice.

A shadow blocked out the sun as something fell towards them, knocking Lyraca off Lynx.

"Gotcha! You thought you could escape me, Lynx! You never will hide!" Artaois sneered. Opening his jaws, he clamped on to the nape of Lynx's neck and began shaking him vigorously.

"I wasn't trying to escape you! What did I do to you?" Lynx shouted, trying to hold down the panic he felt, longing to run.

All three tumbled over each other, growling, snapping. Lynx, not used to fighting, felt helpless. Lyraca, noticing Lynx didn't know what to do, shifted into full werecat, no longer a sleek, half animal, half human, but now with rippling muscles, long jagged canine teeth and sharp, triangular face that was neither feminine nor dainty. It gave Lynx a wake-up call. Seeing her unsheathe her claws, reminded him to unsheathe his, too. Lyraca jumped on the bear's back, shaking him, snarling, growling, causing Lynx to notice more changes in her that weren't as he expected a female to be. Then again, he hadn't been around his kind to see females and males fighting other animals. Any concerns for her change he had to push aside for now and get his mind in this. The fight had to be between him and that bear. Making himself larger by raising his fur up, he braced himself to get in the fight.

Artaois let Lynx go, "You're going to let a female fight your battles?" he growled. Turning to her he said, "What's your problem? My gripe isn't with you, female! It's with Lynx! He's heading to the village! I must stop him! Humans are disgusting animals! They'll hurt him – like they did before!"

"Wrong! Artaois! Ohanaians didn't hurt me! You don't know what you are doing! You don't remember!" Lynx fired. "Leave Lyraca out of this. I can handle you!"

Lynx crouched down and sprang on top of him, digging his claws into Artaois' shoulder and sinking his teeth deep into the bear's other shoulder. The bear roared as he shook himself to dislodge both werecats.

"Female! Leave me alone! My complaint isn't with you!" he brought his back legs up as forceful as he could, throwing her off. She tumbled away but scrambled to her feet as quick as she could and ran back for another go when she heard wings beating fast as a shadow came over them. She looked up and then covered her ears with her paws to block out the sound.

Once Lyraca was cleared off, Artaois shook Lynx off. He landed on his side, and Artaois put a massive paw on Lynx's belly, digging his claws into the tender stomach while grasping Lynx's throat with his powerful jaws and biting down.

An ear-splitting shriek brought the fight to a pause as all three looked up to see a bright white bird descend onto the battlefield. Geoffrey backed winged, his front feet out in sharp talons positioned to adhere to the bear's back. Once he had him, he flapped as hard as he could to take the bear up as high as he could.

Once up high, he flew off with him towards a body of water that was across the mountains from them. Once over it, he let the bear god go and watched him as he roared and tumbled heels over head all the way down. Once that was done, Geoffrey landed besides the two werecats.

"I gotta keep on an eye on you, Lynx. You two left before we could come out to speak. Wayohm wanted to come with me. I had a feeling that bear would be tracking you once I heard Soul Healer say he was linked to you," Geoffrey said.

"I'm glad you didn't bring the otter," Lynx said, licking his sore paws, but every movement caused him to wince in pain. He was bleeding from the nape of his neck, with smaller bite wounds on his throat and side, but he couldn't reach those places.

Lyraca crept up to him, put a paw on his shoulder, leaned forward and began to gently lick the wounds, cleaning it. Lynx winced and tried to back away.

"Hold still, silly. This will help the healing. At least until we can get Soul Healer to treat it."

"Fine! But I don't have to like it!" Lynx protested. "It hurts."

"It will hurt worse if you don't let me clean it," she nudged him.

"Hmmm!" Lynx grumbled. *She's sending me mixed signals here.*

The sky darkened as yellow and light green clouds drifted over the sun. Geoffrey scanned the sky, narrowing his eagle eyes, his thoughts far off. Letting out a sigh, he looked at the two werecats. As he considered the female, he thought he saw her briefly shift into a male physical shape, and then back to female. Wagging his head, he thought that couldn't be right. But werecats can shift into anything, Soul Healer told him before he left to find Lynx and his new friend. Geoffrey suddenly realized Lynx was falling for Lyraca and he didn't know about her shifting genders. Suddenly, he was aware she was staring at him, abruptly bringing him out of his reflection.

"Excuse me, griffin, why are you staring at my tail? Hmmm?"

Geoffrey felt the heat rise from his neck to his cheeks. He looked away.

"Well, what do you have to say for yourself?" Lyraca demanded.

"I was just wondering if werecats shift genders or once a cub is born one gender, do they stay that?" Geoffrey asked. "You know, you're so much like the felines back in Xander's world. Most people think a feline is feminine until they go to the vet and find out their adorable Loitita is a feisty Lloyd," Geoffrey said, thinking fast.

Lynx sat up, snarling. "What you talking about, Geoffrey? Are you accusing Lyraca of not being a female?" He bared his teeth.

"It's okay, Lynx. You weren't raised with us. You vanished as a cub. Stolen by someone from another world. You aren't familiar with werecat ways," Lyraca patted his shoulder in a condescending manner.

Lynx hissed, but stopped, when he noticed the wily smile Lyraca gave him as she pouted, leaning her head to one side as she pronounced each word slowly.

How dare you speak to me like that! He growled, "I'm not a cub!"

"No, but you don't understand, little runt," Lyraca swished her tail and flung her head, her mane moving as if she had long, silky strands. She looked Geoffrey in his eagle eyes, "We are assigned one gender at birth, griffin. But some of us rather flow to other genders when need to be. After a fight, my gender fluidness tends to blend before resettling into the female form, I'd rather be. When I fight, I shift into the male because they are stronger, fiercer and most other animals respect me more."

Geoffrey narrowed his eyes, thinking of Sarah Johnson. She wasn't afraid to fight, and others respect her just fine. "You don't have to be a male to fight well and be respected. Lynx and I have a friend back home that was born female and she stands up quite well in a fight. And she still can be gentle, when she needs to be."

"But Sarah isn't human, Geoff. She's has her Murdoc magic. All Murdoc women are stronger than the men," Lynx reminded him.

"Well, true. But the point is, Lyraca, you can be a female and still be a good fighter when you are protecting yourself and friends."

"Maybe. But you don't know us werecats!" She turned her head away from Lynx and Geoff, left Lynx's side and started on forward. "Come on, it's getting late. The village shops will be closed if we don't get there before too late."

Lynx and Geoffrey hung back, watching her walk away. Lynx lost his desire to go to the village. Geoff turned to him.

"Why are you two going to the village?"

Lynx shrugged and exhaled as he tossed around what to say. "I heard a voice inside of me directing me to go there. I thought maybe I could meet someone who remembers me and can tell me about the wagon Tarrier found me under." He took a deep breath and let it out slowly, then shook his head, "But I don't know anymore. Soul Healer said Tarrier didn't find me under a burning wagon. He said a bear with fire jetting out of his paws set me on fire. It doesn't make sense. Why would Tarrier lie to me?" He looked at Geoffrey, searching his friend for answers.

"Don't look at me. I didn't know you or Tarrier until Prince Tayson brought me to Kent for training. You were almost a year or two old, I think. You looked like no animal I've ever seen before. You were one of a kind. Curá didn't have werecats. Prince Tayson asked Tarrier where he found you, and he said you found him. It was a vague answer. But here, you are meeting your kind. I hope we can find answers."

Lynx's heart fell as his thoughts swam in many conflicting directions. "Why would Tarrier lie to me?"

"I didn't say he lied to you, Lynx. I'm just saying there is more to your story than what he told you or anyone else." Geoffrey's eyes showed he felt bad for his friend. "Come on, we need to catch up with Lyraca. We can talk more."

"What do you remember?" Geoffrey added.

"Not much. I remember from my dreams as a cub, my older brother chased me out of a cave after he beat me up bad. I remember a bear yelling at me. Chasing me. I don't know what else. I vaguely remember seeing two men off in a distance. I think the bear caught me. But I remember being scared more by the bear and running faster. Or trying to. I was small. I was a runt. My older brother didn't want me because he said I didn't deserve to live, and the food was scarce."

"But that was from your dreams. You don't remember anything for fact, do you?"

"No. Tarrier said he rescued me from under a burning wagon. I was hoping to find someone in the village who remembered me. But I don't know. I've changed. . . "

"What do you mean, you've changed?"

"I don't stay in my original form. Tarrier said my original body would scare people because it had scars from being burned and an injured ear from someone biting part of it off. He taught me to hide my true body so others would accept me." Lynx sighed. "Manx says that's why he doesn't like me. I have to be in a body that appeases others instead of myself."

"Do you like looking like a Maine Coon?" Geoffrey asked.

Lynx thought about seeing the Maine Coon form in the Reflection Pond at Curá and smiled. "Yes, I like it. The Reflection Pond showed it to me." He remembered praying to Albagoth for direction and half wished he could go to a Reflection Pond to ask questions. "I wonder if this world has something like that Reflection Pond where I can ask to see my true form."

Geoffrey scanned the sky, hearing birds singing and calling overhead. "Soul Healer or one of the other werecats spoke of an initiation – walking through fire- you haven't had that. Perhaps you will find your answers once you are initiated."

Lynx shrugged. "I don't know."

They walked in silence. Geoffrey replayed Lynx's words and offered his own silent prayer, *Dear Grandsire, please direct me. You always had the answers. Can you please have Albagoth guide us? Not sure if Albagoth will listen since Lynx is a fugitive. He did steal the keys to the Shadowlands . . .*

"I returned those keys, Geoffrey. The Supreme Crow Court Judge cleared me of the wrongdoing because I helped Sarah a year ago. And because I helped catch the Raven. Don't keep judging me on one wrong choice!" Lynx shouted, narrowing his eyes as he walked faster.

"Hey, how'd you know?" the griffin asked, stunned.

"You spoke under your breath, just loud enough that he heard."

Geoffrey turned to see Manx.

"Where did you come from?" Geoffrey asked, looking to his left.

"I was granted a way to portal to places. Sage Tomás showed me how to do it. Anyway, I walked silently behind you two to listen. Hey, where did Artacis go? I have to find that bear before he causes more mischief." Manx said.

"I dropped him off over a body of water. He attacked Lyraca and Lynx."

"I was afraid of that."

"Did you know bears in this world hunt in packs?" Geoffrey asked.

Manx shook his head. "No, but Artaois found his family. That can't be good."

"But it can't be all bad. Maybe they can help him, so he no longer is hunting Lynx. We need to find out why that bear is so focused on him." Geoffrey glanced at the snowshoe lynx to see his wagging his head 'no.' "Why not?"

"Because Artaois is a freak of nature." Manx knitted his brow, letting out a frustrated growl. "I mean, all of his kin believe they're gods. In my meditations, I've been shown that in this world all the bears believe they are the gods of the animals. But the werecats don't follow them nor will they bow down to their rule or supremacy. They follow the teaching of All That Is. And the bears teach their young that werecats don't have souls. But when Artaois was a young cub, he saw Lynx's spirit floating above them. Ever since, he somehow has always been able to spot Lynx. The only time he lost contact with Lynx was when Artaois was sent to Xander's world in their forests. And Tarrier ended up taking in a burned, helpless werecat who was afraid of his own shadow."

"So, you know the pieces to Lynx's early life?" Geoffrey's hopes were up.

"I think I know. But Albagoth won't tell me. The messages I'm given say to allow Lynx to find his own answers. Lynx must want to know. Also, I'm here for Artaois. That bear is supposed to be my student. But I'm assigning myself Lynx, which the Sage may not like. I need to keep him safe. This can be a dangerous world."

"But you don't like Lynx," Geoffrey stated. The albino griffin turned to his friend, noticing Manx was shaking his head.

"No, I do like Lynx. What I have problems with is that he doesn't own his true body and soul's mission. And most of the werecats here take on that true form and nature, but Lynx was supposed to stand out as the extreme. He started out a runt, who was uncapable of becoming what the others were. Deep down, Lynx needs to see those traumas and make amends to his inner werecub for not protecting him better. Tarrier, for some reason, decided for himself, that he had to cover it, so he used his alchemical skills to weave a cushion or glamour to bury those hurtful memories. He also taught Lynx to shift, and to cover his ugly scars so no one in the Kingdom of Kent would be frightened.

"Sage Tomás tried to warn Tarrier that was dangerous. But Tarrier didn't plan on Lynx leaving Curá nor getting in trouble with the Crow court," Manx looked at Geoff.

"We have to help him. . ."

"Correction, Geoff, you have to help him! I am just his guide," Manx turned his head away and perked his ears up, listening to something that the griffin couldn't hear. "I've got to go. The spiritual leader of the Ohanaian Village is calling to me. I'll be in touch. But please, do not reveal any of what I told you to Lynx. And keep him grounded. He doesn't have time for love and mates. Especially the one known as Lyraca." With that Manx paused, closed his eyes, adjusted his inner vision, opened a portal and stepped through it to another part of the world. Geoffrey could see a large camp with people cooking, and a bear approaching.

He shivered. Adjusting himself, Geoffrey looked ahead, to see where Lynx was, then half ran and half flew to him.

Chapter 13

Artaois rose out of the river, steam rushing out his ears, "How dare that freak of nature! That half-bird, half lion stops me from teaching that horrible werecat a lesson! And how in the hell did its ancestors link up with create his kind?" he bellowed.

The birds and waterfowl who roosted in the tubal plants that grew in the river flew at the same time to avoid the angry bear. They chirped a warning to those in the trees to leave, too. They knew it would be dangerous to stand up to the bear god.

Once out of the water, Artaois shook himself, spraying water all over. He stomped off the bank to find some grass and then plopped down, rolled onto his back and wiggled around to finish drying off.

"I despise getting dunked when I don't need a bath! How dare that thing attack me! Just wait till I get my chance to teach him what I can do with my godly powers. Now because that Lynx distracted me, I missed my breakfast! Venison would have been a tasty meal. Especially after that sleepless night I had!"

A slight breeze blew, ruffling his damp fur, sending a shiver up and down his spine. But it also brought a scent of a fire somewhere cooking meat. Following his nose, he walked up an incline and down the other side until he spotted a small gathering of Ohanaians sitting around a fire. There were a few others in the back by their wagons and a table. It looked like they were preparing some root vegetables and berries, Artaois guessed. Squinting his eyes, he wasn't sure what gender the Ohanaians were since they all looked alike to him. The taller ones looked sturdier, even though their hair was longer and pulled back. Some of the shorter ones had facial fur. Artaois couldn't understand how the Ohanaians survived since most of them had exposed skin – they covered themselves with fur; he growled as he recognized some of them were wearing bear skins.

"Those are my kin!" he growled lowly, quickening his steps. The men and women looked up at him. Some grinned. Others went for their weapons.

Artaois flashed to being a cub, spotting hunters poised to kill his mom. He remembered how his sire rose to his full height and swiped them away as if they were dying tree trunks. He didn't give them a chance to hurt his mate. The memory inspired and gave him strength. After all, bears were the gods of the forests, not Ohanaians. And the Ohanaians needed to recognize their supremacy.

Artaois neared the group. The taller, more muscular Ohanaians, grabbed spears while the shorter, stouter ones, cowered in the back. Some went back to the cooking fires while others took up the knives they were using to cut the root vegetables. Artaois laughed to himself. *I have them right where I want them.* One of the Ohanaians gave the war cry as she rushed him. He leapt, too, striking the spear out of her hand. He landed on top of her and began chewing on her throat. One of the men, by the fire cried out, taking up a spear that was in the fire holding the meat. He ran at the bear god.

"This is so easy," Artaois grinned; clapping his paws together, fire erupted from his paws. He threw a ball of flames at the man, igniting his facial fur. Another thought quick and tossed a bucket of water on him.

A majestic Ohanaian woman walked out of the trees, drawing Artaois' attention. She appeared to glow as she walked towards him, brandishing a golden medallion of a small circle within a larger one with many paths leading to the smaller one. The rays of the bright sun sparkled off it, causing the bear god to pause in his attack. Her jet-black hair and dark tan skin radiated as she walked with purpose towards him. Her people bowed and made way for her. Once she reached him, she held up the symbol.

"Greetings, royal bear. All That Is has a message for you. There is plenty to eat here on Ohana, you don't have to kill Ohanaians for food. All you must do is humble yourself, ask for us for food to fill your empty belly and we will be happy to share. We respect all animals and people," she said.

Artaois shook his head, and spat at the mention of All That Is. "All That Is said that to you? I am the god of this world. My tribe rules the animals and nature. Where is All That Is? And why can't I see this so-called deity?"

"All That Is is all around you. Inside of each of us and gives us to share with others," she said.

"I don't take hand-outs! You all killed my kind to keep yourselves warm! Who are you to say bears don't count?"

"I never said bears don't count. I merely included them as being part of All That Is. We can work together. . ."

"Work together? Me? Working with humans? Humans almost killed my mother when I was a cub before that demon werecat came into my life. But after my sire killed them, I saw the soul of a werecat. My sire said they were soulless and demons! Ever since, I remember him and have vowed to keep him away from humans. But a strange half eagle, half lion attacked me a while ago when I was on his scent . . ."

"Enough! You are the one we've been waiting for. You are Artaois. You have missing years here. So much has changed since you've been gone."

Artaois' lower jaw dropped, and all his thoughts spilled out along with his anger and hunger. A fly buzzed around him zipping into his mouth, landing on his tongue, then beckoned others to come in where it was cool. Artaois took a deep breath, inhaling it, then started coughing before it could slide down his throat.

Finding his voice, the words rushed out, "You've been waiting for me?"

Manx strolled out from behind the holy woman as she said, "Sage Manx has instructed me to keep an eye out for you. Only we weren't expecting you to be on a warpath of destroying my tribe as we prepared our midday meal. Which you are more than welcomed to share in."

Artaois snarled at the sight of the snowshoe lynx, "What are you doing here? And how is it this human can understand me?" Staring down the snowshoe lynx, Artaois didn't get a response. Spotting the so-called sage give a wily grin, while glancing at the Ohanaian woman holding the symbol in her hand, started the bear's blood boiling when he noticed she smiled back at Manx.

"You two are conspiring against me! You want to destroy me!" Artaois roared. "I will tear both of you

apart and roast your dead bodies for my breakfast!"
He broke into a run and jumped the fire pit, only to
have the holy woman hold up the hand that held the
symbol and a bolt of lightning issued from it, hitting
the bear god in his chest, tossing him to the side like a
wet towel.

Feeling his spirit rise above his body and
surroundings, Artaois saw the campsite, noticing
there were other people and animals beside each of
the humans and one by Manx, too. They appeared to
be guiding and protecting the people they stood by.
One of the spirit guides knelt next to a human that
Artaois remembered trying to kill. They looked up at
him and pointed. One of the spirit guides came over
to Artaois, "No one is against you, Artaois. But you
are going to destroy yourself if you don't stop chasing
the werecat and threatening the Ohanaians. They
aren't your enemy. And Lynx isn't your enemy,
either," the spirit said to him.

Artaois wagged his head. "I don't understand." He
paused to replay what he just heard. "I mean, I know
Lynx isn't my enemy. I want to protect him. Someone
had been beating up on the poor cub. I was certain it
was the humans. Or Ohanaians. But I don't
understand." He glanced around himself and at each
person and Manx. Noticing the bright colors around
each individual, he felt blown away. "What are those
colors? And who is the person with that circle within
a circle?"

"She is the holy one that represents All That Is. Her
name is Shalom."

"Peace." Artaois didn't know how he knew that, but
just saying made him feel like someone turned a light
on inside his being, even though he was out of his

body. "Who are you? And what are those colors around each person?"

"I am the One Who Guides. On some worlds, we are called Spirit Guides. But here we are just called One Who Guides. We wait on each person we're assigned to."

"I have one?"

"No. The bear tribe have rejected the guides on this world because they believe themselves to be gods. Only a few of the animals recognize them as such. And you bears, I mean no offense, really do not help the other animals. Instead, you all rule as dictators and act like everyone owes you the worship and adoration. You all have to earn it."

"But Manx has a guide –who looks to be human . . ."

"Manx has two guides. One is of physical form, whom isn't here with him and an animal guide who is with him always. Manx has one because he is aware of his spiritual self and his training as a guide to all travelers who beckon to him to him requires it."

"Colors. What do they mean?"

The Ohanaian the spirit guide was nursing moaned and called out.

"I have to go back to my student. It's time for you to return to your body, Artaois."

With those words, the guide pushed his spirit back towards the unconscious body.

Artaois' eyes flew open; taking a deep breath, he became aware of the holy woman and Manx leaning over him, whispering.

"His colors are dimming," Shalom said. "We need to get the healing broth ready."

"It's being done, your Shalom," another said behind her.

"His colors are brightening," Manx spoke. "He saw the spirits. That wasn't expected. Few do see them. I wish Lynx could become aware of them."

"Lynx will in time, Manx. All That Is says to be patient. Artaois is your student, not the werecat. Soul Healer will assist him."

"Missing time, though. . . and how did Artaois and Lynx become linked like they are?" Manx twisted sideways at the same time bringing up his left back leg to scratch his behind his ear.

"We aren't the ones to tell you, Manx. Right now, it's this bear we need to focus on," Shalom said then held a finger to her mouth, meeting Artaois eyes as he stared at her.

"Who are you? And what did you do to me?" Artaois demanded.

"I'm Shalom. Holy One of the Ohanaian village. "I prevented you from hurting me and my people. You're here to learn more about who you are and how we can assist you, though, it isn't my place to deal with you. Your real teacher is Soul Healer of Werecat tribe. Manx will take you there. First, sit up and we will feed you."

"Werecat! No soulless werecat will teach me anything!"

Chapter 14

Dark clouds rolled in front of the sun, enveloping the trail in darkness, as the winds increased. Rain began to drizzle down on the travelers. Lynx hunched up his shoulders; shivers rippled up and down his spine. Geoffrey spread out his wings and shook the onslaught off him, sending the fleeing streams of cold water to the werecat.

"What happened? Where did the pleasant day go?" Lynx complained.

"Not sure. But hope this isn't an indicator of how depressed you are -like in Curá's Senilona desert."

"No, I doubt that," Lynx frowned. "Besides, I'm not depressed. Just merely astounded that you would accuse Lyraca of being a male!"

Lynx paused. Each step sent sharp quivers of pain sheering through his system; he winced and whimpered. Blood loss was also catching up with him.

"Where is Lyraca? I think she abandoned us," Geoffrey accused. "Isn't she supposed to be escorting you to the human village?"

"I can't go on much further. I need to rest," Lynx found shelter under a large tree. He panted, "The pain is too much."

Geoffrey approached him to examine his wounds, "We need to get you to the town to get a healer." He glanced around, squinting to see if he could spot Lyraca anywhere close. "You stay here. I will fly ahead to find that werecat and bring her back. If I can't find her, I'll fly into the town to find a healer myself."

Lynx nodded, his head swimming, he tried to lay down and he felt the ground underneath rise to meet his side. It scared him, so that he just collapsed but felt someone caught him and gently laid him down.

Once down, he sighed, his mind spinning, replaying all that happened. Geoffrey accusing Lyraca of being a male – or able to shift from female to male- the thought of that being true rubbed his fur the wrong the way.

Lynx struggled to stay conscious but had an overwhelming sensation of rising out of his body, floating above it and noticed the semi-conscious body of a Maine Coon laying there by a large tree root that appeared to be creeping towards it, poking and prodding it. Lynx turned his head to the side, trying to understand what he was seeing – the Maine Coon didn't look right. It wasn't just the deep gashes on his throat and side where the bear had done its best to snap the poor animal's neck. He also saw something more – deep within the glamour, Lynx knew that body had to go. There was a demon deep inside – but it wasn't just a body that looked like a demon – the heart was pure gold. Mischievous, magical – but this poor animal hadn't even touched on all the magic that was his to live.

"Werecat known as Lynx, come with me," a deep, resonating, musical voice summoned him. Lynx turned toward the voice. It was the spirit of the tree.

"Who are you?" Lynx asked.

"I am Methusla. One of the Wisdom trees that Albagoth uses to teach and lead."

"Am I dead?" Lynx asked.

"Do you want to be?" Methusla replied.

Lynx smiled and let out a chuckle. "I don't know. Artaois sure wants me dead."

"No, Artaois is confused. He wants to protect you, so in wanting to protect you, he thinks he must hurt you. The danger he perceives is confused with so many messages his parents taught him before the portal was opened to throw him out of this world. Albagoth did that to protect all werecats. In this world, Albagoth is known as All That Is. Artaois believes werecats don't have souls, but he sees your soul/spirit, and is conflicted."

"All living animals and beings have souls," Lynx replied.

"Yes, you have a seed knowledge. You can learn. But first you need to open yourself up to the truth. Follow me," Methusla turned as if in stop motion – Lynx followed, realizing all he had to do was decide to go forward and he floated after the large, majestic tree spirit.

"Where are we going?" Lynx asked when he caught up to the old tree. Lynx noticed rings around a stump on his side. He guessed a sturdy limb had been cut off or broken off in a storm. Remembering Tarrier saying trees showed their years on a land by the number of rings, Lynx guessed the old tree must have been one of the original ones that Albagoth had planted when this world was created.

"We're going underground, so I can show you plans. Demons are born in fire, Lynx. You don't remember the fire that scarred you. The human that took you from your birth world, Ohana, thought them ugly. Your pride healer would've shown you how beautiful they are. Fire is what you must go through once more to see the whole plan."

"Albagoth's plan?"

Methusla laughed deep, his leaves sounding like chimes, "No, Albagoth oversees the souls as they plan their life in a body. You chose some of what you have experienced."

Lynx replayed those words, not sure how to react. Images came to mind, then he remembered standing before Albagoth last year after he had been sentenced. Albagoth appeared to him as a werecat unlike anything he'd ever seen – triangular face, short hair that stood up in spikes, with part of an ear missing and burn scars down one side and his tail all crooked. Lynx was puzzled. Albagoth's words were cryptic. The Creator of All Worlds was genderless and species fluid- often appearing to mirror how the person or animal looked in order to assist that person to relate to and feel comfortable – but Lynx had never seen a werecat that looked like the Spirit was showing him. But the form repulsed him. It was ugly, scary, and filled Lynx with terror.

"Remember, Lynx. Remember. Little Runt – your story is still unfolding. People of the Land will have the answers you seek. Leave Curá and Tarrier now. This part of your life is done. Follow the Indigo Travelers. Take on your Mantle. Embrace the fire. Embrace the demon. Embrace who you are meant to be."

With those words, Albagoth transformed into one tall being without gender identify or species identifier, took a deep breath and blew him back to the body.

But that was two years ago.

"What questions do you have?" Methusla looked at him, bringing Lynx's attention back.

Lynx's spirit shrugged, not sure what to say. Tarrier's face and his shop back in Curá came to mind. He remembered being a helpless cub – kitten, Tarrier called him- and hearing him uttering some spells in another language. The Wizard Seabon assisted him. Lynx remembered Tarrier saying, "You are pretty now, Lynx. You will be able to speak clearly and shift into any form. It is better to take on the body of a household cat, but you are better than any housecat because you are more magical and able to transform things. I will teach you. Only, you do not use that magic without my guidance. Others will fear you once they realize what a werecat is. I tell them a werecat is another breed of household cat. You are one of a kind. There are no more like you."

Another time, Tarrier told him not to worry about where he came from or what his early years were. But fire always both fascinated Lynx and frightened him. Once, as a kitten, watching Tarrier forging swords for the new soldiers in Kent's Kingdom, he remembered seeing a bear calling for a werecat runt. The flames formed that bear, and it scared him. Tarrier laughed it off.

"There are no bears in Curá," Tarrier laughed his deep, belly laugh. "No such thing as a bear. You have quite the imagination for a young one. Forget it. That is a waking dream."

Lynx shook his head. "Why would Tarrier lie to me? Why would he put a spell on me to block out my early years? And why would I choose to have that done to me?"

The old tree raised a slender branch, with one smaller twig pointing up. "That is a good question. Only you can answer it. What else do you want to know?"

"Why does Artaois want to hurt me?"

"Come, we will explore that," Methusla said.

Lynx glanced around, sensing more swirls and wind tossing him, blocking his way to follow the old tree. "Help, something has me!" he called, feeling something latch on to his back leg, pulling him down. Lynx twisted around, to see a dark cloud holding him back, trying to keep him from following.

Methusla turned around, called on the directional winds to pick up as he stretched out several branches, the ends morphing into hands, "Be gone, evil! This werecat is not yours! His soul belongs to All That Is!"

"Not if I can help it. He seeks to thwart the bear I've enticed to do my bidding. This werecat is mine! Was mine as a runt and will always be mine!"

"I was never yours!" Lynx roared. "I don't even know who you are!"

"I am the force that will prevent you from ever taking on your true form! I am the force that resides in your nightmares, that fuels Artaois and encourages him to use his dark spells to hurl you into horrible tailspins! Once a demon always a demon!"

"I've never been a demon! I've never hurt anyone and seek only to help others," Lynx roared.

"You lie! You're a self-seeking, werecat who doesn't even remember your birth form. You hide from your true knowledge. It will never be yours!"

Lynx abruptly brought himself up on his hind feet, spun around to face the dark force, hissing, snarling and spitting. "I know nothing about what you are speaking of! Since when was I self- serving? Since when did you own me? I don't even know who you are!"

The dark energy swirled into arms and legs with narrow eyes with infernos burning deep inside. Lynx could feel the heat, reminding him of the teens' high school bon fire a week ago. "You really don't remember?"

"Enough! Lynx was a young cub, Ember. You didn't have a chance to grasp onto Lynx like you have others of his kind. In truth, no werecat has been pure demon for eons here on Ohana. You had your chance, you thought. But Lynx got away from you without even trying. You took control of Artaois, believing he could assist you. Indeed, you do have Artaois' soul. But that can be changed," Methusla admonished. "This is not your time. This is Lynx's time to discover before the healers find his body and call his soul back."

"Werecats have no souls!" Ember shouted. "I'm the one who taught the bear gods this. Werecats are demons! Born in fire! Lynx, you must go through the fire to become what I know you will always be!"

"No, no! Never!" Lynx turned to the wisdom tree, "Teach me about being a werecat! Tarrier kept my true form and nature away from me. Help me to rediscover this."

"Yes, that is what we are in the process of doing . . ."

A strong force yanked on the cord that attached Lynx's soul to his body, before he could hear Methusla finish – sending him hurling tail over head back, slamming him hard inside his body.

Images of Lyraca swimming, shifting from a petite boned, shapely feminine part human part werecat to a large, triangular face, full werecat with large shoulder and hip muscles, that cried loudly of being masculine both intrigued and frightened him. *Lyraca, what are you? You are the bitch of my dreams. But you aren't a female. Soul Healer said you weren't what I thought you were.*

The visions shifted to a tree urging him to fight going back to his body, urging him to dig deeper into his memories, speaking as if the rivers were rising to drown out the urge to become fully grounded yet.

"Lynx, are you okay?" Geoffrey's voice echoed through the fog.

"He's still fighting the dark force spirit of the fire to survive. Give him time. The fever is taking him," came another voice, that Lynx couldn't place. "Assistant, come put some more cold packs on him and change his bandages. The Ohanaian healer and Manx will be here soon."

"Come step back, Geoffrey," Clarence said. "Let them work.

Wayohm came forward, "I wish I had been with you. I would have tripped that bear up! He will pay for hurting Lynx!"

"Wayohm, that's a good thought, but you're so little . . ."

"Don't underestimate me just because I'm small! I can fight and use my size to my advantage!" the river otter asserted. "I'm small, but mighty."

"Yes, you are," Soul Healer patted the otter on his head. "I don't mean to patronize you. You have a strong soul and pure purpose. You see more in your visions than most of your kind do. When you get back home, others will look up to you and you can teach them. For now, we all need to step back and wait for the Ohanaians to come to us."

Lynx saw himself walking towards a man whose back was facing him. Glancing down at his paws, he noticed his legs were slender, grey and black with orange intermixed. He had six toes, counting the opposable toes. He released a sigh, grateful he could still open his own milk bottles, but he didn't recognize his legs. His bones were larger, stronger and sturdy. His attention refocused on the man. As he grew nearer, the man turned around, and he could see it was Tarrier.

Narrowing his eyes, Lynx fumed, "Tarrier, you hid my memories! You blocked what really happened. I demand you unblock them now! Or explain yourself."

"You're in no place to demand of me. Without me, you would still be a runt without a home. Or a dead runt. I saved you from the inferno. Homeless – your tribe didn't want you! Your older brother bit your ear off and wanted to tear you to pieces. That bear cub demanded he get you instead. Vengeance, Lynx. It wanted to prove something to his people. He was on fire, but he survived. Fire – Lynx- walk through the fire!"

Lynx turned around to see others around him – villagers from the Kingdom of Kent, with torches - "Set it on fire! Demons love fire! Burn, evil one! Through the darkness, through the heat!"

One lone person with a hood on stood out from the rest, Lynx turned to see the him removing his hood to reveal it was the Sage of Stillness, "Lynx, the truth is yours once you are well. Tarrier did what he did against my direction. Werecats walk through the inferno of initiation, don't be afraid. Your true self isn't who you think it is. And it isn't who others say it is. You will find it when you willingly go through the inferno on your own."

One must follow the darkness to find the light, my precious werecat. You were loved.

Lynx looked around but couldn't see who said that. The voice reminded him of his mama's.

Blinding white light with a black oval in the center shone and illuminated his way. In the middle, like a pure black iris, it urged him forward. Lynx plodded on, unsure where it would lead. An inner voice said, *Speak to your soul, Lynx. Invite your soul in. Trust your soul to know what is best. Trust your soul to be working with All That Is. See the path clearly.*

As he walked into it, he saw the sign:

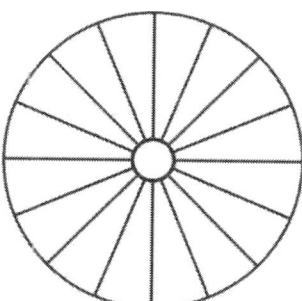

Lynx held up his head, putting one slender foot in front of the other and headed towards the dark center, which grew blacker till it appeared purple.

Overhead, from somewhere distant, he heard, "We're losing him. Come on, healer, where are you?"

Chapter 15

Artaois stomped through the dry grass, snapping at the bugs that pestered him. Dark clouds rolled in, further dampening his view. Those stupid humans in this world thought they knew it all. In addition, Manx, who was supposed to be his teacher, sided with them.

"Growl! Who do they think they are to ignore me? Would anyone dare treat a god that way?"

"You aren't a god," Manx replied. Artaois turned to stare him down.

"Where did you come from?"

"I've been walking beside you since we left the Ohanaians campsite. Their healer was called to the werecat cave.

Artaois wagged his head, "Why can't I just be left alone?"

"Because then you won't ever remember the truth and know how you and Lynx became connected. You weren't intended to end up in the World of Nampa in their forests. Your soul's purpose was to stay here and learn to use your abilities to teach your people to follow a different path – away from godhood."

"How do you know so much about my soul's purpose?" Artaois sneered.

"I'm apprenticed to a spiritual healer/traveler. I've sat at the spiritual feet of All That Is more times than I can count and have access to many of my student's soul records in the Library of Lives back in the Crow Court Realm that is above the world of Curá."

Artaois tossed over those words. "Crow Court Realm? Other worlds? And one god rules them all?"

Manx smiled. "In your view you can say that. Albagoth is not a ruler. Albagoth is a spirit without body, gender or species. One can say it is species and gender fluid. It takes the form of whatever is standing in front needing its attention and counsel."

Artaois thought about that. "Have I ever stood in front of this being?"

"Maybe you have. I can't say. I'm not allowed to accompany my students to the Spirit realm. Your soul goes alone."

"Soul? You mean spirit?"

"It is the same thing, Artaois." Manx looked at him, seeing his energy and muscles were rippling with each stride, instead of being so taut like a top that was ready to be released to spin out of control. "You look more relaxed. How are you feeling?"

"You gave me a lot to think about. I'm thirsty and my stomach is growling. Where are we headed to?"

"Over to yonder stream. We can catch some fish. After we eat, we will rest and continue. I thought we would stop at the werecat's cave so we can check on Lynx and consult with Soul Healer. You and Lynx have to work together to get your memories back."

"Ah – no—I can't. I mean, werecats don't have souls. So . . ."

"Correction, all living things have souls, Artaois. Albagoth created it that way."

Manx looked at the bear in the eyes to see they were as big as two round river stones and his jaw was wide open just waiting for flies to come in. "That surprises you?"

Artaois closed his mouth. "Shocked! Dadpa said no werecats had souls because they were devils and played in fire. But I was sure I saw a young werecat cub out of its body. I wanted to send it to the animal afterlife because it was stuck. Next time I saw it, it was in body and running away with part of its ear bit off."

Manx leaned his head to one side, then straightened up and looked at him, "Your sire needs to learn, too. All species and living things have souls. Including werecats."

"Don't down talk my dadpa! He is a noble bear and knows everything! He loves me and taught me all I know!"

"Really? He loves you?" Manx challenged him.

"Yes, he does."

"Then why didn't he give chase when you went after that werecub who was injured? And why didn't he go looking for you after you disappeared?"

Artaois stammered, muttered a few words, but none of them made sense.

"Why did you give chase to the wounded runt of a werecat cub?" Manx drilled.

"How did you know it was a runt?" Artaois' eyes widened.

"And how did you know that runt became Lynx?" Manx interrogated the bear god.

"I'm not sure. Something – the fire that jets from my paws somehow linked us together. When I landed in a different world and he wasn't there, I forgot all about him. I forgot this place. I forgot my sire and dame." Artaois stared out, hearing a bird's shrill call from above distract him. He watched the bird fly off, following the drifting clouds as all his words vanished with the cloud clusters. A light breeze had broken them up. A bug landed on his nose, he shook it off, remembering what they were saying.

"I don't know how to answer you, Manx. I don't know what you want from me. All I know, once Lynx came into my world, back home, I remembered the wounded runt and that I needed to warn him. I thought I could help him – give him a soul or something." Artaois' eyes showed his hurt and sadness.

"You can't give someone a soul they already have. Lynx didn't need another soul. He needed healing. Instead of helping him, you set him on fire," Manx accused.

"No, no, no—it was an accident. He was going to the Ohanaians – the humans. They're dangerous. There were two of them that were trying to reach him. I had to get there first. – One of them had a large sharp object strapped to his waist. I had to prevent them from hurting him worse."

Manx smiled.

Both animals stopped walking to listen to each other-facing each other, Artaois saw the snowshoe lynx smiling.

"What did I say? Your smiling- laughing at me. Was what I said funny?"

"No, not funny, Artaois. Your memory is coming back to you." Manx stood, "Come on, let's continue our journey to the river. We don't have to talk."

Chapter 16

The darkness increased the further he walked; no thoughts entered his mind. Wonder and curiosity filled him – awe. Turning slightly to look behind him, Lynx wondered where he had been. No memories remained. An image of a tree formed in his mind.

What was the name of that tree? Where am I? Who am I?

Why am I here? I must be dead.

"Come, little runt. Walk towards this voice," a voice called. Lynx couldn't see who was speaking.

The image of a tree and a teen age young lady wearing all black clothes with black and white striped hair, two piercings in her lower lip, a symbol of Albagoth on her forehead and army boots stood by an ancient tree. A large spider stood near her.

"Don't worry, Xander. We will find him," said the young girl.

As if he was floating above them, Lynx saw two teen young men, sitting. The one with black hair and fair skin had tears streaming down his face.

"I hope so. It isn't like Clarence to go off like this. But we knew Lynx was depressed and scared. Geoffrey said an otter appeared from out of nowhere," Xander wiped the snot that was dripping down his face.

Milo patted his foster brother's back, "You said you saw them go down the middle stone. Clarence said it was a portal. So did Geoffrey. They will come back. We always came back from our journeys. So, this is

Lynx's turn to learn who he is and find out why that bear is trying to hurt him."

Nickoli raised up, "Albagoth will be guiding them. Sage Tomás promised me when he came to me the other night before they vanished. I know you will worry, Xander. Just know they will return. Manx is with them."

Those forlorn teens vanished, bringing the werecat back to his journey. *Who are they? And why are they worried about me? I guess I'm Lynx.*

Taking a deep breath, he let it out slowly, wondering where this dark tunnel would end.

"You are almost to the end, Lynx. Before you get to me, remember who you are and what you are supposed to be. The way you appear to others is not how you started out. Your present perception of self was formed by someone who was afraid of your natural persona. He managed to re-program you without your permission. I didn't tell the Crow Judges to deal with him because it had to happen as part of your soul's development. It changes now. Lynx. Do you want to know who you were meant to be?"

Lynx squinted. Shrugging his shoulders, another sigh escaped from his lips.

"I don't know who I am. Who are you? And why can't I see you?"

Shapes, grey and dull white, faded in, zipping around him. One landed on his nose and began playing with his whiskers.

"Spirit whiskers are the most fun," the sparkling light chirped. They're more flexible and not as sharp."

Lynx puckered up and blew air at the sparkling ball of light.

"You don't play fair! No fun! You used to be fun!"

"I don't know who or what you are," the lost werecat said. "Pesky thing! Go away!"

It darted away.

Dark shapes, some pure grey and others striped grey and white, swam around him morphing into images, like birds, trees or fish. Others just floated, morphing into bubbles being squeezed in the middle, with one bulbous circle on the bottom, like a lava lamp or becoming an infinity shape – floated, drifting and moving as if they had no care in the world. One swam close to the werecat, resting on his nose. He blew at it

"You're breath stinks!" The shape uttered. "If I had a nose, I'd be plugging it with my fingers."

"What're fingers?" said the other bubble attached to it.

"Not sure. Not sure what a nose is, either!"

"Go away!" growled Lynx.

"Come children. Stop bothering the lost werecat. He's here seeking my help," said the voice that was beginning to sound very feminine.

"We want to help, too!" chirped the lights and the bubbles together.

"Not now. None of you are old enough to take form nor enter a body."

"I am," said one brave light. "I want his body!" The light formed a hand and finger pointing.

"It isn't nice to point, young one. Yes, you are almost ready to enter a body. But Lynx's body will be occupied soon. Be gone!" the voice commanded. A loud snap or crack echoed through the tunnel and the shapes and lights disappeared, leaving the frightened, curious and annoyed werecat in total darkness.

"Why is it so dark? Why can't I see you?" Lynx asked after a while. He sat down, his legs felt weighted down, and the air seemed to close in on him.

"You have to go through the darkness to find who you really are. To remember."

Lynx glanced around. "Remember. Remember what?"

"Fire. Fire burns bright. Fire . . ."

"Burns! Sears! Scars. Hurts. Blisters and leaves lasting marks. But I have none."

Another voice called out, "Don't be too long in this place, Lynx. Otherwise you will forget you have a body and the people who love you and miss you."

"Albagoth?" Lynx asked.

"Yes. I am they," answered the second voice.

"Then who is the other voice?"

"Listen. Continue to stroll through the darkness. This second voice will reveal itself in time."

"Time has no meaning in the eternity, dear Albagoth. Also known as All That Is. All that matters, is getting this wayward werecat back on track to become what he was thwarted to become," the second voice said.

Thumbs. I have thumbs. Lynx paused, sat down and lifted his right paw. *I'm in spirit. I can fly. I'm magical. I can call on the light and float out of here.*

That tree – what was its name? Methusla? I can ask for Methusla to assist me. Or Albagoth.

"Not this time, Lynx. You must go it alone. But call on your Soul. Call on the Wisdom Trees. Spirits good and bad. Even the bad spirits can assist you. Above all, trust yourself."

Lynx felt the presence of the Creator of All Worlds retreat from around him.

Odd. I didn't feel that presence until they left. But somehow, I feel a sense that I can do anything.

Lynx saw a memory of himself standing before Tarrier, explaining his idea for his opposable thumbs. Tarrier put him to sleep, but it wasn't sleep – hypnosis. Snapping his thumbs, Lynx remembered the words Tarrier, the alchemist blacksmith from Curá used. He then remembered Soul Healer saying Tarrier triggered Lynx's werecat shifting abilities to create the thumbs.

I didn't want to believe it, but it's true. Tarrier lied to me. Tarrier hid his knowledge of my magic – only telling me what was safe.

What am I to do about this second voice? Who is it and how do I get it to reveal itself to me?

Snapping both thumbs on either front paw at the same time, Lynx said, "Bring me to the light!"

All at once, he was out in the open. Bright sun shone a brilliant green garden with vivacious trees, flowers and butterflies of every color and decoration flying and drifting around. Some landed on the roses to drink deeply the wonderful nectar inside them. Others played tag with their friends.

Glancing around, Lynx saw a medium height woman with a black, red and white striped hair. But she had cat ears. And her round face with slanted eyes, twinkled knowingly, yet there was something off about her.

"Who are you?" Lynx asked. "If you don't tell me, I will use my magic to discern or make you tell me."

"I'm Lilith. The first woman that Albagoth created for the promised garden. Because I was equal to man, I was cast out. No man could control me. Men fear what they cannot control."

"I don't fear you. I only fear what I don't understand. Why have you brought me here?"

"I haven't brought you here, dear Lynx. You brought yourself here. You do know your body is dying, right? You seek answers – but are afraid of what you will find.

"Your friend, Manx, believes Soul Healer will help you in your journey. He trusts that werecat spiritual leader to help the errant bear who believes he is equal to a god. He knows nothing about creating worlds and assisting others for good – he only believes he can punish you for trusting humans. As a runt – you went through a fire that was wrongly thrust upon you. As a grown werecat, you have a choice to go through the right fire to become what you were destined to be."

"What was I destined to be?" Lynx asked. "I was a runt whom my oldest brother, Claude, wanted to die of hunger because he couldn't kill me. He almost succeeded. I escaped with my life. I don't remember much – but was told about a bear – I mean"

Lynx shook his head, all his thoughts, images and memories assaulted him at once, he needed to clear his mind. He took a deep breath and let it out. "I mean, I saw visions of a bear cub with his paws on fire running after me. He pounced on me, set me on fire and then threw me into a wood pile."

Lynx paused.

"I didn't remember all that. I don't know where it came from."

Lynx realized she was grinning, tapping her foot impatiently with her arms crossed in front. "Hold it, that doesn't feel right. I mean, who really are you and are you here to help me? Do you work with Albagoth?"

Lilith stopped tapping her foot, uncrossed her arms and nodded. She walked towards him, slowly she began to shift into a feline form, with a triangle shaped head, large ears and long saber tooth teeth on either side of her jaw. Still walking on her hind feet, she grinned.

Lynx's heart thudded, as he felt his spiritual fur standing, creating a larger body than what he had. His primal instincts kicked in, it was either fight or flight. His eyes narrowed, and then shifted into large round circles, deep yellow with slender irises.

"I asked you earlier who you thought you were supposed to be. Your true body, personality was tragically altered the day that both that bear and that human from off the Ohanian world interfered in your soul's lessons. You didn't give me the correct answer. Only half an answer. You don't remember the two humans who stood by, observing you and that bear cub fighting, do you?"

"Wah-wah – haw- wh-ah- t – what are you?"

"I am Lilith! Goddess of both the underworld and the overworld. I share creation – my Tarradonnas are both good and evil. Some have broken from me and only respond to Albagoth. Others see the benefit of working with both Albagoth and me.

"You, Runt Lynx, were supposed to become a demon! Be a curse to your society! Thwart the likes of your brother, Claude, who plays both ends of the stick and at the same time, won't play by either rules. You are demon! But you were denied the true fire of initiation that would have allowed you to choose your own path. Now you walk around wearing a shell of a pretty boy, bringing dragon's blood swords to spoiled Indigo Traveler boys who are also lost to the true meaning of what it means to be an Indigo teen-ager!

"You live with humans and are lost to your true werecat nature!" Lilith raised her hands, which became claws, like a demon. "You didn't have the choice! I give that choice! Become that demon you were supposed to be!" She reached up to the sky, closed her clawed hands and thrusted them downward. All sunlight vanished, plunging the meadow into darkness as thunder shook the ground and all around them. Lighting flashed, striking the nearby tree.

Lynx turned tail to run away, only to feel something scratchy grab him and lift him up.

"You're okay, Lynx," Methusla cooed softly in his ears. "Go back to your body. It isn't your time. Lilith can't hurt you."

"I'm not afraid of her. I'm curious, how do I talk with my soul?" Lynx asked, trying to stand up in Methusla's palm shaped leaf.

"You are soul, Lynx. You are soul within a body." The tree paused to consider. "Well, right now, you are a soul without your body. First lesson, your soul retains all memory of what your plans were for this life. Your soul can guide you to know how to relate to that bear god and to know how to understand Tarrier."

"What about Tarrier?" Lynx inquired.

"What do you want to know or ask him?"

"Why did he lie to me? Why did he cloud or suppress my memories?" Lynx said without thinking.

"Snap your toes, little Werecat," the old tree directed. "But first you need to pop back into your body and take it with you."

Lynx nodded in agreement. He lifted his paws, snapped his thumb and first toes together thinking about his body. Once he entered, he opened his eyes, glanced at everyone standing around, some with tears streaming down their faces which changed when they saw he woke up.

"What's wrong?" Lynx asked.

"You were dying," Geoffrey said with soft keens and deep breaths.

"Dying? No, it isn't my time. I'll be right back." Lynx lifted his paws and snapped again, thinking about Tarrier in Curá and vanished again, not taking time to say "bye."

Alchemist blacksmith Tarrier stood inside his stone house adding small logs to the fire to warm it up. The nights were getting colder now, even though the day orb still rose high in the Curá sky. The old man took a deep breath and then let it out as he slumped his broad shoulders, his mind reviewing his younger years.

As a young man, he dreamed and wished to follow the wandering ways of the spiritual travelers. The one before the Sage of Stillness used to travel to his world. He'd listen with wide eyes, to the stories and lessons of Spiritual knowledge. He wanted to learn and was eager to see other worlds.

He meditated, studied all his tutor assigned him and prayed for the day when he would be assigned his own mentor to travel with. The day came. He was assigned to a young spiritual traveler, named Sage of Stillness – Sage Tomás. The first world they went to was called Ohana. Sage Tomás translated the name to The Land.

It was a land of werecats – shapeshifter felines with triangle faces, slanted eyes bright like a blacksmith's furnace on high and misguided bears that believed they were gods who ruled the land.

Deep down, Tarrier made a poor judgment choice, and got himself kicked out of the apprentice spiritual interworld missions. He interfered with the wild life that he came to help.

"Lynx, I'm sorry," Tarrier sobbed, kneeling down by the fire, bending over. "I lost you. I should have left you where you were. And allowed others to care for you."

Tarrier wasn't aware anyone had entered his home without coming through the door to overhear him.

Lynx observed him, not knowing what to say. Then he felt a presence beside him, glancing over, it was Manx.

"I came to support you, but Tarrier won't see me nor sense me. Tarrier is a broken man. Since you've been gone, his life has gone downhill. He's lost the support of the King Tonyar due to illness and the Prince is being prepped to rule once his father is unable to handle the duties. And he misses you terribly. He believes you left him because he wronged you."

"He did wrong me. He hid my memories and altered my natural state. He also lied to me, saying he never has been off of Curá. That just isn't true," Lynx hissed.

"Direct your ire to him, not me," Manx advised.

Lynx nodded.

"What are you sorry for, Tarrier?" Lynx demanded.

The alchemist blacksmith jumped up, turned around and yelled out of fright. He turned around and saw the tall werecat he'd known since he was a cub.

"Lynx, my assistance and pet! You came back to me!"

"No, I didn't come back to you. I only came back for answers. I left because if I didn't, the Superior Court Crow Judges would have sentenced me to wander the Senilona desert because I violated their trust. It was far better to go with the Indigo Travelers to their world than submit to the punishment."

"Now, I'm back – briefly, to learn the truth! You didn't find me under a burning wagon, did you? You lead me to believe that burning wagon was somewhere here on Curá, but it wasn't. I was the only werecat this world has ever seen. I want the truth! Why did you steal me from my home world? And why did you wipe my memories and prevent me from knowing who I really am?"

Lynx's words, said in anger and anguish, became sharp knives that penetrated deep into Tarrier's heart.

"I don't know," Tarrier said. His eyes retreated deep into his sockets, as new tears rose behind them. Tarrier fell to his knees.

"You must know," Lynx approached him. "You found me when I was young – what? I'm guessing about four months old. I vaguely remember fighting with my older brother, Claude, and him chasing me out the cave. My ear was bleeding . . ."

Tarrier shook his head, holding his head in his hands. "I can't keep re-living this! That is the one moment of my entire life I totally regret. It's caused me so much grief."

Lynx walked in front of him and put a paw on his shoulder, "Tarrier, I don't know what happened to you. But meeting you has been both a curse and a blessing."

Tarrier continued to cry. He muttered something, but Lynx couldn't figure out what he was saying.

Lynx looked around the small, familiar home. It brought back pleasant memories of roaming the rooms, sleeping on Tarrier's bed, or lounging on a rug in front of fire listening to Tarrier reading from books he got specially delivered.

Lynx paused, cocking his head, "Where did you get those books? No one else in this world has books like yours. Everyone else has scrolls or gathers in the courtyard to listen to the traveling bards.

"Where did you get those books you used to read to me?"

Tarrier stopped crying. "You never noticed, did you?"

"Noticed what?" Lynx said. For a moment, he narrowed his eyes, seeking to see deep within his former friend and some would say, master. "You aren't doing very well since I left, are you? There's more going on here than you have ever told me."

Tarrier's face flushed, ashamed. "I never shared with you who I was. I had to hide my past from you. I pretended to be someone I wasn't, denying how crushed I became. I hid your memories so you wouldn't become what I was told you would become if you ever could walk through the fire of your initiation."

"I've been hearing about that. But how did you get to Ohana? And what does that have to do with the books you used to read to me?"

Tarrier stood up, "I need some tea and a biscuit." He headed outside with a large pail to get some water from the well. Then he turned and really looked at the werecat.

"What happened to you? Your neck is bleeding. It looks like a bear mauled you."

"Yes, a bear god mauled me. He's been sending enchantments to me ever since he realized I was back in his world. Somehow, he landed in Xander's world and found me. We are now in Ohana. I need answers.

I need you to unblock my memories and tell me the truth." Lynx said.

"Yes, I will tell you the truth. I will also treat your wounds."

"And stop feeling sorry for yourself!" Lynx ordered.

"I have done so much wrong! And now Albagoth is punishing me for it," Tarrier sobbed as he went out of the room.

Lynx turned around, shocked to hear him say that. It occurred to him that Albagoth isn't the one who is punishing him. He's doing it to himself.

The solitude of the fire, drew him in, Lynx felt himself drawn into it, visions of playful werecat cubs frolicking and a bear chasing him – panic-stricken, and a sharp penetrating stabbing sensation made him jump, startled, as he became aware of a wet substance dripping down his chest. Sinking to his knees, Lynx brought up a front paw to check the stabbing pain on his throat. Once he brought it away and examined his pads, he saw the bright red, sticky substance and brought that paw up to his mouth to lick it. It tasted of iron. "Blood. I'm still bleeding."

Weakness took over; Lynx laid down on his side, "Methusla, why did you want me to have my body here when it is dying?"

Closing his eyes, he saw the old tree and heard it say, *We brought you this far, Lynx. Listen to us. Tarrier will not let you die. Allow him to make this right. Allow him to heal you and take off the barrier to your memories. Your time isn't over. Continue to seek your soul to fully come back from. Part of it still resides in place where souls plan for their next life.*

Are all souls returned to the life of the species they start in? Lynx asked, as he felt his spirit rise once more from his body.

"No, not always. But I can't answer that for you. I've always been a wisdom tree, planted here in Ohana at the time of the land's first creation, said the ancient tree.

Banyan tree, Lynx thought.

As he drifted, his awareness expanded to see in the werecat cave, Manx was talking with Geoffrey, Soul Healer and others. Another werecat, with rippling muscles, a cruel sneer and one broken saber tooth, as well as a scar down his ugly triangular face stood there. Lynx didn't know him, yet something about the way he moved reminded him of Lyraca, and how she shifted to fight Artaois.

Lynx observed all of them and heard Soul Healer call the new werecat Claude. Artaois entered from a back room, and they all stated Curá was their next destination.

No, no, here. They can't come here. This is my time –

Lynx's second awareness observed Tarrier come in with hot tea and warm cloth dipped in healing herbs. He began to wash and treat Lynx's wounds.

"Yes, this is your time. But you aren't going to die. You have a fever, little one. But I'm a skilled healer. Rest. Drink this to lessen the pain," Tarrier kneeled beside him. "When you aren't delirious, we will talk."

"No, tell me. Answer my questions. I hear you, Tarrier. I trusted you. You violated my trust," Lynx's uttered without breath.

"You were a helpless, wounded cub. A bear with paws on fire was chasing you. I had to intervene. Though, my mentor cautioned me not to. I disobeyed him. I knew once that bear caught you, he would rip you apart. I felt sorry for you."

"My people – My sire and dame—they would have looked for me."

"No, Lynx. They would not," Tarrier said. "You know in your heart. I could see your panic. Rest, Lynx."

Lynx pulled away from his caregiver's gentle cleansing, wincing in pain, whimpering.

Tarrier lifted the bowl of tea to Lynx so he could lap up some of it. Lynx could taste the chamomile, rose fruit and lavender. After he had his fill, he sighed and lowered his head down, drifting off to sleep.

Lynx drifted above the room, hearing voices and saw a figure approach him. As the figure neared, he saw it was a young Sage Tomás of Stillness.

"You're ready for your apprenticeship, Tarrier. You passed all your exams and Healer Astral said you understand not to interfere with the animals on the worlds where we will be visiting and teaching."

"Yes, I understand. But I heard you have children on another world. How is that not interfering?" Lynx heard himself say.

Odd – I am inside of Tarrier's body. Yet I am still me. How is that possible? Lynx thought.

"I fell in love. The woman I fell in love with was not one of the animals. And she hid her pregnancy from me until the boys were toddlers. She didn't want to marry me. I visit as often as I can."

"What happens if I do interfere?"

"You will be terminated from the apprenticeship. You better have another occupation in mind." Sage Tomás pronounced each word with emphasis through set jaw.

Lynx felt Tarrier's heart drop to his stomach and his breath catch, realizing this wasn't a rule to test.

Their first two worlds went well. The next one was called Ohana – Lynx looked through Tarrier's wide-eyes, as he saw this new world, with many interesting animals he had never seen before. Werecats, with large ears, triangular faces, two saber-like teeth, long sleek bodies and narrow eyes. Tarrier thought of the eyes burning with a fire.

"Devil cats," Tarrier said when Sage Tomás and he were alone.

"Devil cats are born in fire. Werecats, when they reach a year or two, walk through a fire to become what they are meant to be. The devil cats. They take their name afterward. Not all become a devil cat – Some are healers – a few become ambassadors to the Ohanaian clan. We will meet the Ohanaians later."

Tarrier, in the silence that followed, considered the werecat, with his evil looking face which sent tremors of terror through his being, imagined a werecat being all evil. He feared for his life. Though, he knew cats back home were magical on his home world – not Curá

As they sat by their fire, Tarrier watched the day fade to darkness, seeing a large mammal lumbering along with two cubs behind. The adult mammal rose on her back feet and roared. Tarrier's hair rose on the back of his neck.

"What is that creature?"

"That's a bear. They live here. They believe they are gods and rule the other animals. They don't fear humans – or Ohanaians. Ohanaians seek to live in peace with them."

Tarrier let that sink in, awed by the height, the massive bulk of the animal. He observed the bear approach a tree, put her front paws on it and begin to push, and bounce leaning all her weight against it, until finally, the tree snapped in two. The tree wasn't a young one – it looked sturdy—but that animal was able to push it down as if it was a sapling.

"Tomorrow we travel to the Ohanaian village to meet with their town leaders and spiritual representatives," Sage Tomás said as he stood and stretched.

Tarrier picked up a twig and started peeling the bark off. "Do they recognize Albagoth like we do?"

"They recognize All That Is. Remember, all paths lead to Albagoth. It doesn't matter what they called. It only matters we listen to their stories of the creation of the world and we share our stories of creation of other worlds. We are not here to convince them our way is right. It is the spiritual lesson – what you send out is returned to you twenty-fold."

As Sage Tomás spoke, Tarrier observed a young cub approaching them, listening to their conversation. Tarrier noticed that the bear cub seemed to understand what they were saying. He shook his head from side to side, saying he disagreed.

The bear cub's paws were large, so Tarrier guessed he was about six months old. The cub lifted one paw up, shook it and a flame appeared on top of his pad, burning bright, but didn't seem to be burning him at all.

"One day, I will set all Ohanaians on fire," the bear cub said. "They tried to kill my momma. Dadpa killed them and we roasted them alive and feasted on their scrawny bodies. Ohanaians do not worship us. They need to bow down to us. We're superior to them. And you two," the bear cub stated.

"Artaois, come here this instant! Leave those fools alone!"

The cub's words sent chills up and down Tarrier's and Sage's spine.

"Yes, momma," the bear cub turned and rejoined his momma and sibling.

"It talked. I didn't expect that bear to speak."

Sage Tomás nodded. "The animals on your world speak, too. You just have to learn to listen."

Lynx realized, as he observed the young Tarrier and his mentor heading into their dwelling for the night, that Tarrier came to Curá from a different world to study with Healer Astral. That world was very different than Curá in that the animals there didn't communicate. Though, Lynx couldn't find the name of that world. It was locked deep within Tarrier's memory.

The next day, Lynx observed the two men setting off for the village. Ohanaians were a tall people with all color ranges depending on how long they were in the open air and what they ate. The Land itself was rocky, with steep mountains, with few trees. Thick vegetation near the caves where the werecats had their dens showed the trails they had carved out.

Tarrier heard hissing and growling coming from one of the caves as they passed it, mixed with guttural voices and a young werecub hissing and snapping back.

"Ignore it," Sage Tomás advised. "Most likely one of the older cubs is teaching a younger one to behave."

Tarrier's attention was drawn to the fighting – he fought the impulse to intervene. But he listened to his mentor.

Roads appeared and they saw wagons and people on horses or horse-like animals.

Off to the side they saw two adult bears with their cubs walking away from them.

"That's interesting. I didn't expect the bears to be coming this close to the village," Tarrier said.

"They don't. Something is wrong here," Sage said, with concern. At the same time, two men came to the spiritual teachers.

"You must be Sage of Stillness and your apprentice," said one of the men, who stood about as tall of Sage Tomás but was stocky and muscular due to the heaving of heavy hay bales.

"Yes, we are. This is my apprentice Tarrier originally from the World of Mylar. He studied on Curá which answers to the Spiritual police called Crow Judges," the sage explained.

"It's unusual to put birds in charge of spiritual law."

Abruptly Lynx's spirit was yanked out of Tarrier's body and dropped into the runt Werecat cub's body.

"Runt, I'm talking to you! You better behave! I'm going to rule you!"

"Stop hiding who you are, Claude! Stop beating up on the runt just to prove you aren't gender appropriate!" said another were sibling.

"Shut your yap! Torrind! You know nothing!"

"I know more than you think I do. I heard your discussions with Soul Healer in your preparing for your Fire Walk. You to be the new ambassador to the Ohanaians," Torrind snarled.

Claude back pawed him, sending him flying against the cave wall.

Furry and anger surged through the runt's blood. He snarled and hissed, tried to say, "Don't manhandle Torrind like that!"

But it came out, "Rowal! Grrr myhanlde!"

Claude laughed, mimicking the runt's speech. "You can't even talk. You're old enough to. Some magical devil cat you will be."

Runt grew to twice his size, snarling, hissing – lowering his back legs and focused on his target. He sprung at Claude, landing at his throat, sinking his baby teeth deep into Claude's main arteries and did his best to shake the larger brother.

"You're a pest Runt! You'll never be a killer!" The larger werecat lifted a front paw and knocked the smaller one down as if he was a flea. "You don't deserve to live! And we can't afford to feed you!"

Claude held the struggling runt down with one massive paw. "Stop struggling. Let me put you out of your misery! You will never make it to your Fire Walk. I will see to that!"

Claude lowered his head, open mouth, large saber teeth sending Runt's fight or flight instincts through the roof. Claude took a hold of the Runt's left ear and bit down hard on the side till blood seeped into his mouth. He ignored the Runt's whimpers and cries. Once he knew he had successfully managed to break off a chunk of the ear, he let go and chewed it up, leaving the Runt with half of his left ear.

"Leave! Runt! Escape this place! If I ever see you again, I will tear you apart limb for limb and feed you to that bear cub that follows you wherever you go!"

Runt, terrified, ran from the cave. He ran so fast he didn't know where he was or where he was heading. He passed two strange Ohanaians wearing robes and walking with long wooden poles.

Closer to the village, the Runt hoped to find a healer. He didn't know how, but he knew the Ohanaians had healers, like they did. Then the bear cub and his family caught sight of him, smelling the blood trail of his wounded ear.

With the village in sight, Lynx/Runt, knew he could relax. Noticing the two strange travelers were now talking with Ohanaian villagers, he wondered if they would still take notice of him. Only the adult bear began calling to the errant bear cub.

Runt's heart rose to his throat as he saw the bear's paws were on fire as it ran in full sprint.

"Now's my chance! I have you, Runt! I will teach you we bears are gods to you soulless creatures! I will reform!" the bear cub shouted.

The closer the bear cub got, the hotter and stronger his fire burned.

"Stay away from the Ohanaians! Only I can save you! They tried to kill my momma! They will kill you, too."

The four men paused in their conversation to watch the spectacle. Runt noticed that the younger of the men in a robe started to run towards the Runt, but the older one put a hand on his arm to stop him.

Runt turned to head towards the four men, hoping for help. At the same time, the bear cub pounced, picked him up in his inferno paws and held him.

"I got you, you soulless demon! I am your god! I can give you the soul you lack!"

"Fat chance!" Lynx spoke through the Runt's young voice.

Artaois heard his parents calling him, but he ignored them. Startled to hear the runt taunt him, the bear cub hurled a ball of fire at the Runt as it ran towards a wood pile, setting the whole pile and the wagons near it ablaze.

Again, Lynx's spirit awareness was split. His runt body screamed and yowled in pain as it burned, the putrid aroma of burning fur rose above, spreading throughout the village as others came running to watch the spectacle.

Another part of him watched Tarrier break away from Sage of Stillness, "I have to do something. I can't stand by to watch an innocent werecub die a fiery death!"

As Tarrier ran, he took off his robe, stripping down to his cotton peasant shirt and trousers. Noticing a bucket of water meant for the farm animals, he grabbed it and threw it on the fire. Adrenalin surging through his body, not feeling the pain of handling the burning logs and planks, tossing them to the side as if they were feathers.

Artaois growled and roared with anger. As he ran towards the man helping, not hearing three pairs of feet were running after him.

Lynx observed another man join Tarrier who was throwing another pail of water on the fire to keep it from spreading and a woman came with a blanket. Another woman came with an extra blanket.

Sage of Stillness reached Artaois, held his hand with the palm up facing the bear, "You've caused enough trouble today, bear! You're expelled from here!" Mumbling some words, the sage opened a portal in front of Artaois which he fell through.

After the fire was out, the Ohanaian native reached the burning werecub. Lynx's spirit rested back inside the runt's body, he screamed and whined in pain. His tail was badly burned as was his left side, which was where most of the flames licked him. But he was alive.

One of the women came forward holding an extra blanket, asked to take the cub. Once given the cub, she wrapped him gently in the blanket.

"He needs to be treated," Tarrier said. "I have training in healing burn wounds. My father was a blacksmith and my mother was the village alchemist on my home world."

"Aren't you from the world known as Curá?" one of the Ohanaian men said.

"No. I moved there to study with Healer Astral and the Superior Crow Court Judges. I'm from another world called Micha in the Andrés galaxy," Tarrier explained.

"Do they recognize All That Is?" asked one of the women, who was wearing the Albagoth symbol, like Sage Tomás'.

"Yes, we do. All Paths lead to All That Is. We may have different names for them, but we all know they are a genderless creative spirit that created all worlds," Tarrier replied.

The woman holding the werecub handed him to Tarrier.

"Poor runt. What are you?" Tarrier asked. "What is your name?"

"He doesn't have a name yet. Werecats are supposed to walk through a fire and not be hurt. Only he's too young."

"No, that bear cub was bewitching him," said one of the men who had met the Sage and Tarrier. "I've been aware of him taunting and following the cub for a while." He turned to the Sage. "Where did you send him?"

"I sent him to another world in the Milky Way Galaxy, hoping he wouldn't find this cub once he recovers," Sage said.

But as Artaois flew through the portal, a small piece of his soul split off and landed inside of the runt. It would rest there, asleep. It was awakened once Lynx ended up in his new world.

Lynx's consciousness returned to his present body, where he rested comfortably. Gradually, he woke, aware that there were many eyes observing him, talking in hushed tones.

"I wasn't planning on entertaining so many," he heard Tarrier say. "Especially meeting you, wise Soul Healer. I heard of you when I was an apprentice to the Sage of Stillness but didn't get a chance to meet you."

"Indeed, I heard of you, too. You were the one who was banned from Ohana because you took the burned werecat runt from our nest. The right thing to do would have been to return him so we could heal him and teach him to shift. Instead, you stole him, changed him for your own selfish reasons and out of fear of what he would become," Soul Healer chastised him.

"I lost a lot when I made my decision to take the runt. I was warned." Tarrier hung his head. "I didn't know how advanced Ohana was. Nor did I realize that the werecats were so evolved. I heard the fighting . . ."

"Unsupervised cubs will fight. The older one who chased Runt out has been dealt with. He was taught not to bully those who are younger and to be more supportive of those that are slow to learn."

Lynx opened an eye to see Tarrier looking humbled at the older werecat. He noticed Geoffrey, Clarence and Wayohm there, too. Off in the far distance, Artaois laid stretched out like bear rug on the floor, away from the others.

Lynx's eye contacted Geoffrey's. He quickly closed it.

"He's awake," Geoffrey cried.

Tarrier and Soul Healer abruptly turned to look at their patient.

"No, he isn't," Tarrier said.

Clarence, "He's faking it. I know Lynx." The white and orange domestic short hair feline approached the patient, "Come on, Lynx. We know you're awake."

Soul Healer chuckled, "He did that as a cub, too."

"He's better. Look, the color of his face is returning," Wayohm cheered.

"I'll be the judge of that," Soul Healer approached Lynx, putting a gentle paw on the patient's nose.

Lynx lifted a paw to brush it off, and then sneezed.

"Come, my little Runt, you're no longer sick. Your memories will return to you. Your soul is almost whole."

Lynx opened both eyes and yawned. "Oh, hi, guys. Where did you all come from?"

"Lynx, you faker! You know we came here from Ohana! Manx transported us. We were worried about you." Wayohm wiggled over to Lynx, stood up on his hind legs and put his front paws on Lynx's bed. "Look, Artaois even wandered into the cave, looking for help. He isn't sorry for what he done, but he wants to make it right. He realizes part of him is missing."

"Missing? What do you mean part of him is missing?" Lynx sat up abruptly, then winced and cried in pain, but angry that Artaois was missing a part, remembering he was also supposed to be missing something.

"Careful now, Runt. You are getting better, but your stitches won't hold for long if you move too fast. Tarrier sewed up for me," Soul Healer said. "Lay back down." The old werecat looked at Tarrier, "Please go get another bowl of that herbal tea and a light meat and vegetable snack for Lynx to nibble on."

"Be right back," Tarrier excused himself, wanting to be helpful, but resenting being ordered around by an animal.

"You said there is still part of me missing," Lynx asked. "How can Artaois being missing something and not me?"

Soul Healer leaned his head to one side, considering, and then straightened it back up, mulling it over.

"You're missing your memories, which are returning. Once you go through the fires of initiation, you will be uniting with all yourselves," Soul Healer explained.

Lynx let out a low growl, frustrated by all the talk about lost memories and so on. He wanted to get up and move, pace, or just get out of here. He tried to get to his feet, Soul Healer pushed him back down.

"You know, I really hate just laying here on my side. I want to get up. Move around," Lynx tried to move again.

"Wait till Tarrier gets back. He can assist you better." Soul Healer cautioned. "Yes, there is. First, before I tell you. What did you remember?"

"What do you mean what do I remember?" Lynx furrowed his brows and narrowed his eyes.

"Your soul went on a journey while you were unconscious. You relived much of your early years. You still have questions."

Lynx shrugged his shoulders, trying to brush it off, replaying much of it. "How do you know what I experienced?"

"I'm a trained spiritual healer, Lynx. I can see spirits and know when someone has a soul that is traveling or when part of your soul has escaped to a safer place. Tarrier interfered with your development. Haven't you felt like part of you was lost? Or locked away?"

The tip of Lynx's long, fluffy tail stood up and dropped with a thud. Then went up and thudded down again as he thought, staring off in the corner of the log house, watching a fly buzzing around.

I never felt like it before, he mused. But everything that has been happening has caused me to wonder. Tarrier betrayed me.

"I re-lived some of Tarrier's earlier years. It was like a dream. He studied here with the late Healer Astral, Geoffrey's grandsire. But he isn't from Curá. I always thought he was raised here. But once I got back, I realized he had books – like what Xander and Milo collect back on Nampa World. No one else here as them. How did Tarrier get those books? And why did he betray me?"

Tarrier entered the room with a tray of cheese, hard bread and carrots sliced into small pieces for everyone and herbal tea bowls for everyone, except he had a cup of tea for himself.

Handing a bowl to Lynx, he helped his former assistant up so he could lap some up. Lynx managed to sit up without hurting himself more. Clarence, whom had never had tea before, found the taste odd.

"Are you sure felines can drink this? My staff just gives me water. She heard that we felines couldn't have cream or milk, but you put milk in this," Clarence stated. He licked his lips.

"This is fine for you, Clarence. I studied many different animal medicines when I was younger. My mom was also an animal doctor on my world of origin. I helped her growing up, so learned much," Tarrier said. "But we didn't have mythical animals, like werecats and griffins on my world. I only heard the legends about them before Sage Tomás and I traveled to Ohana. I made many errors. One was not finding out the truth behind the stories. It cost me my dream occupation."

Lynx wagged his head. "Maybe so – but that doesn't answer one of many questions I have. Why did you alter my memories so I wouldn't remember where I came from or who I was?"

"I did it to protect you. You were young, had ugly scars and couldn't sleep because of the nightmares of that bear chasing you with its paws on fire."

Artois perked his ears, pulled himself to his feet, shook and lumbered over.

"That is my clue to get in on this party," he grumbled. "You, human, brought tea and snacks for everyone but me! Manx made me come here. I am the bear with paws that can call fire. That fire does not burn me. But why say the soulless cub had nightmares that I caused? I only wanted to save him from the humans! I also wanted to heal him, maybe through my godhood I could give him a soul."

"No need to give Runt what he already has," Soul Healer said.

"What? You sound like Manx! Manx tried to convince of the same thing. But I have every proof that werecats don't have souls."

"You're no god, Artaois. None of you bears are," Geoffrey stated.

"How would you know, bird brain?" Artaois taunted, jamming a paw in Geoffrey's chest.

Geoffrey narrowed his golden eyes, brought his front right leg up and knocked Artaois' paw away with such force it made the massive bear flinch.

"I know much more than you about what a true creator or god, as you put it, does and is! My grandsire taught me what it means to follow Albagoth. And Albagoth itself showed me all living things have souls. This includes plants, rocks, mountains and trees," Geoffrey stated firmly. "I do have a bird's brain, but that means I am very intelligent and respect all living beings. Unlike you, bear, who only wants to throw your weight around."

Artaois snarled, lunging at the pure white griffin. Geoffrey spread his wings out to their full twelve foot span, causing those around them duck or be knocked over as he attempted to flap to lift himself up into a fighting mode.

"Enough! I will not have two oversized toddlers fighting in my small house!" Tarrier shouted. "If you two insist on fighting, take it outside!"

Geoffrey folded his wings up and hunkered down, humbled, "Sorry, Tarrier."

"Weakling! Never apologize, griffin! I challenge you to a fight! I challenge you to show me what you know!" the bear roared.

Manx pounced between them to break up the fight.

"Stop it, you two! The main issue isn't who has a soul and who doesn't. The issue is," Manx turned to

Artaois, staring hard into his dark brown eyes, "Is this. Artaois, you keep saying you're a god. Show me! Prove to me you are a god. Create something for us. Or show us how you would give a soul to Lynx."

Artaois' jaw flew open, all bluster and hot air escaped with a hissing sound, reminding Tarrier of a balloon with a slow helium leak.

"Outside?" Artaois muttered.

Tarrier glared at him and the other two, "Outside!"

Artaois closed his mouth with a loud smack and swallowed hard; his muscles in his shoulders and legs trembled.

Manx lead the way. All that could, went outside.

Wayohm stayed by Lynx's side, "Do you want to stay here? Or can you walk out?"

Lynx shrugged. "I don't know. Not sure what the fuss is. All I want to know is why Tarrier hid the truth from me. And why Artaois felt the need to chase me." He brought a back leg up and scratched his ear and the side of his neck.

"Be careful," Tarrier and Soul Healer cautioned. "You have stitches there."

"Yes, I know. They hurt and itch horribly!" Lynx whined.

"It would be a good idea to go out to see what they are doing," Tarrier observed. "I know you have your questions, Lynx. You need answers and I will give them to you. Since you've been gone, I have felt very remorseful and sorry for myself. I realized what I did to you was wrong. I was sure you left because of it. Even though Crow Judge Connor said otherwise."

Lynx half shrugged while considering his words. At the mention of the crow judge's name, he had a renewed concern. "Crow Judge Connor! What if he becomes aware I'm here? Won't he or another crow judge come and hold me accountable? I'm not supposed to be here!"

Tarrier shook his head, "No, because I live in the outskirts of Kent Kingdom now. Even if they do become aware, I will tell them it is only for a short visit. You don't plan to stay."

Wayohm glanced from one to the other and back. Clarence came in to check on them.

"Are you three going to come out? They won't start this until you all come out," the domestic long hair feline said firmly.

"Come on, I will help you up, Lynx," Tarrier put one hand under the werecat and lifted him up. Lynx whimpered, and grunted, but made it up.

Chapter 17

Manx set up a stone ring that was roughly six feet wide and six feet across. Artaois paced from one side of it to the other while they waited for Tarrier, Lynx, Wayohm and Clarence to join them. As he paced, he mumbled, "What am I to do? I know I'm a god, but Dadpa didn't teach me enough about my powers. I'm self-taught. I know to use spells and incantations, but I know nothing about creating souls or people." He sighed. "I know how to influence animals to obey me – except for that blasted river otter and werecat. And that griffin and . . ." he glanced nervously at Manx. "What if I can't prove I'm a god? What if I can't prove Lynx doesn't have a soul? What if. . ."

"You fail miserably?" Manx added.

The massive, self-absorbed bear paused and glared at him, "Excuse me! You're interrupting private anxiety mutterings! No one asked you to insert your thoughts!" the would be bear god resumed his pacing, while quieting his inner turmoil to beseech his ancestors for assistance to figure out what a soul is, how to see it and how further how to create it and bestow it on a soulless creature.

It occurred him to sit on his hinny, back legs extended in front of him, back straight and front paws up, with two toes curled together in a circle. He attempted to do that but found out his toes weren't flexible like Lynx's. He sighed. He wasn't pleased. He opted to put his paws together and hum calmly, hoping it would clear his mind. A tiny swirling light came into focus which grew as it spun clockwise. Artaois focused on it.

Wayohm and Clarence came out, stood by Geoffrey and Manx. They asked where Lynx and Tarrier were, then heard them come up. Tarrier was assisting Lynx to walk on his hind legs to make sure his wounds didn't re-open.

They all watched Artaois. Wayohm was curious.

"What's he doing?" the little otter asked.

"Sssh," Manx whispered. "He's meditating."

"Where did he learn that?" Geoffrey and Lynx asked together, then looked at each other, "Jinx. You owe me a soda," they uttered and laughed.

"What's a soda?" Wayohm asked.

"It's a sugary drink that my staff's offspring drink that isn't good for them," Clarence answered. Then added, "Those two are just joking. Xander, Milo and their friend, Sarah, say that when they say the same thought together."

"Oh."

Artaois continued to focus on the swirling circle of light as it grew and began to flicker with different colors that pulsated, vibrating to a soft music that Artaois had never heard before. He swayed, trying to mimic the rhythm and beat. Slowly he sensed his inner spirit rise from his body and all at once, it all went black. A heavy presence encompassed him, and he heard a voice say *What are you seeking?*

I'm seeking a soul for the lost werecat. I saw his spirit wondering lost.

Who are you to request what this creature already has?

No, he doesn't already have it. I am a god! As a god, I need to find a way to create this soul. What is a soul? What does it look like?

The voice laughed. Artaois to roar inside his vision. Who are you to laugh at me? Show yourself! Reveal who you are that speaks to me?

I am the one that created all things! In the world you are in now I go by the name of Albagoth! You are nothing, Artaois. I urge you to go deeper within yourself. Don't call on me until you understand what the nature of who you really are is. Furthermore, each of my creations already have consciousness. Being self- conscious is the soul that survives after the body dies. I ask you, what is your nature?

My nature is – protection, Artaois answered.

Protection of whom?

Um . . .

Wrong answer!

The presence abruptly vanished.

Okay, Artaois considered. Keeping his eyes closed, *I am a god. My dadpa was a god as was his dadpa before him and his momma and my momma. Who is this Alba-gooey to say what I am and what I am not! I create myself!*

Visualizing the swirling circle again, Artaois began to hum the tune he heard a bit ago. *I need to dig deep.* Soon all was black again. He saw himself digging a hole in the blackness, searching for who he is. Searching for the soul, without a body.

Runt, I know you're there. Runt, the injured werecat cub from years ago. Come here. I must find you. A soul without a body. A soul without a name. I will keep you safe. Come to me. I have a body to put you into.

Artaois stopped calling, considering, *What does a soul look like? It possibly is clear, like a phantom. Dadpa mentioned that because he saw one once. But gods aren't supposed to be afraid, so Dadpa found a way to dissolve it. Mamma said phantoms aren't real. But I saw this runt once. I know it was dead – but it's still alive and over there.*

Artaois struggled to open one eye to look at Lynx. But his eyes were shut tight, like a clam that wouldn't open without a strong rock to pound it on. Yet he was aware Lynx was there. He could sense the werecat, along with the others who watched him intently. So, he moved one arm out in Lynx's direction, focusing, *I will bring him here. I will bring whatever is deep inside him that is pretending to be a soul here to travel with me through this hole I am digging.*

As Artaois saw himself squeeze Lynx's chest, he realized that wasn't working since his paw wasn't touching the werecat's body. Instead, he focused on penetrating the chest cavity. He saw his front leg go inside of Lynx, and he grabbed the ghost within the werecat.

Lynx gasped, clutching his chest with his right paw. Geoffrey, Wayohm and Soul Healer rushed to his side. Tarrier stepped behind the ill werecat, ready to catch him as he collapsed on into his arms.

"What's wrong?" Clarence and Geoffrey asked, worried about their friend.

Manx and Soul Healer exchanged glances, nodding as they were talking mind to mind and then nodded. Manx lifted a chin towards Soul Healer. And he responded by shaking his head.

Manx stepped forward, "Artaois has managed to drag Lynx's soul out of his body and make it a part of his meditation. Artaois doesn't know what a soul is, nor does he know how to create it. Albagoth has said Artaois doesn't believe him. So, we wait. Let's allow this and see what happens."

Chapter 18

Lynx's soul, after being yanked out of his body, was pulled towards a black hole, thinking, *I can't allow this to happen again. Methusla, where are you? I need your guidance.*

Methusla? Who's that?

A voice said.

The wisdom tree I spoke with days ago. Who are you?

Lynx turned around to see a large, effervescent bear standing at the edge of a black hole. As Lynx gazed into the hole, he noticed a light peering up at him, beckoning him to jump, like it was saying he was safe.

Artaois? Is that you? You pulled me into your meditation. Why?

Because I need to give you a soul. I don't know what a soul is or what it looks like.

Lynx chuckled. He plopped down, crossing one of his front legs across his chest and resting the elbow of the other leg on the one that was crossed, then rested his toes on his chin and drummed his chin in thought. Pure White light, I call to you, Lynx uttered softly in a language he didn't know he knew. *Assist me to protect what is mine and show this bear who is in charge of me.*

I am in charge of you! The bear god's spirit roared. *I am the one who will give you what you lack!*

What I lack? I lack nothing- except the answers from Tarrier that I came to Curá to get.

You lack a soul! Artaois roared. *I will give it to you. But first, I need to see what it looks like.*

Lynx laughed. *I lack a soul? You are the one that pulled my soul/spirit out of my body. If I didn't have a soul, you wouldn't have been able to yank it out of my body like this.*

Artaois clapped his paws together – the sound reverberated throughout the vast space they stood in, shaking Lynx to his core. He felt like a cartoon animal after cymbals were clapped together over his ears, with his from legs plastered to his sides, stiff as a board bouncing on his back feet around till the vibration went away. After he ceased, he saw the bear has ignited his paws. The bear god grinned, his eyes glowed with reflection from the flames.

I am in charge of you, Lynx! I know your kind. I created your kind. You are a demon. I know the stories. I believe them. Werecats aren't to be trusted. They shift bodies and become evil if not properly disciplined. But your kind fails to follow us bear gods.

That's because we know you bears are not gods. Becoming a demon is a choice, Artaois. You can't give me what I already have. I'm standing in front of you without my body. You should see it. You are seeing it. You touched it. You – hey, what are you doing?

Artaois posed with one leg back leg crossing his body, leaning back, with one front flaming paw behind his head like a baseball pitcher, zeroing in on his target and then uncrossed his leg as he leaned forward releasing the flames. The flames hit Lynx's spirit body, sending them spinning like a top out of view.

Once Lynx's spirit was gone, Artaois shook himself, and opened his inner eyes, blinking. Standing in front of him was a young bear cub, quivering.

Don't hurt me. You've hurt me enough all these years.

Who are you? Artaois asked.

I'm the missing part of your soul. When that traveler hit you with his spell to open the portal, part of me broke off and landed in the runt werecat cub. You don't understand yourself. What Dadpa told us is wrong. Werecats have souls. You aren't complete without me. Us bears are not gods.

I don't understand.

I'm the one who first sighted the werecub's spirit. I'm the one that wanted to help him. I knew he was being abused. I didn't mean for my fire to harm him. With me inside of Lynx, you shouldn't be able to make fire. But you found it. Now, make it right. See Albagoth. We need assistance to get back as part of you.

Chapter 19

Lynx continued spinning and tried to stop by mentally telling himself to stop. *Hey, I'm in control. When I'm in spirit, I have control—like lucid dreaming.* Then he remembered he had learned to control his dream state. And this wasn't a dream state. This was something else.

"Hey! Stop!" Lynx pulled his front legs, positioned his paws so his pads were facing up and snapped his thumbs against the first toe. "I demand to stop spinning!"

Abruptly the spinning stopped, and he fell, exhausted. But the world around him continued to spin for a bit. He felt like he did when he used to chase his tail as a werecub.

"It will pass. Hmm, what does Xander and the gang see in those spinning rides at the fair? Awful! I feel sick."

Once his vision and the world stopped turning, Lynx noticed it wasn't dark anymore. He was in a meadow. He stared a bush that surrounded a cove of trees, thinking he saw something. Someone appeared to be watching him.

Flaming eyes glared out of the trees, hypnotizing those who spotted it in the least expected places. Lynx didn't know who or what they belonged to.

"Are you one of us?" Lynx asked, unsure how to approach the eyes. And more curious as what the body looked like.

"Eyes of fire and brimstone. I am what you are to become. I am one who you are supposed to be. Once bitten, never shy. Not even twice. Go forth, my pet. Walk toward me."

"But why should I walk toward you?" Lynx asked. "I was born a werecat. I wasn't bitten and then became one. Most werecats are born."

"But you haven't gone through the fire yet. That bear prevented you from going through the fire. You lost yourself to the humans. Would've lost yourself to the Ohanaians you were running to after Claude, my servant, scared you off. But that misguided bear god fouled up my plans. He's to blame for this mess. Not Tarrier. He heard lies about us. He heard tales that were so far-fetched he was afraid of what he agreed to take in and then he molded you to his desires instead of you acquiescing to my plans for you. Contrary to what you have been taught, white light doesn't guide you. Black light does. All werecats have a chance to become the demon."

Lynx shook his head, "No, no. That isn't true. Soul Healer didn't become the demon. Neither did Lyraca. . . ."

His words were cut off as the Flaming Eyes roared with laughter. Thunder struck and lightening rent the sky as a bolt hit a nearby tree felling it towards where Lynx stood.

"Lyraca is one of mine, precious Runt. Don't you see? She is of two souls. When she shifts into her fighting form, she becomes the soul she was born as- the one that bit your ear off and used to swing you around by the tail to kill you. She is your friend and ambassador to the Ohanaians, but she hides her second nature. The one nature that would get her banned from their village and excommunicated from the werecat pride. When you get back to your world, you will see the truth. She shifts easily. But for you, you need to face the fire."

Lynx wagged his head, "I went through the fire once. I went as a cub. Artaois threw flames at me, setting me and bunch of discarded wood planks on fire. Trapped. I was trapped there until the Ohanaians and Tarrier freed me. I don't fire anymore."

"This fire is different, Runt. You get to choose who you are meant to be. You get to see the demons which are legend in Ohana. The legend that caused Tarrier to tremble in fear. The legend, Runt is once bitten, the werecub will surely become the legendary demon," the voice continued.

"But I wasn't bitten," Lynx said. "As I have said, werecats are born."

"But you were bitten, Runt. You were bitten by a littermate who was bitten before his fire baptism. He went mad . . . is mad. And tried to rebirth himself which split his soul – no, not split his soul – he was given another soul that was pure – but the two souls fight for the control of the body and the shifts. He will lose to the female, but he is strong. Neither will be accepted after this struggle."

Lynx shook his head, trying to follow the conversation.

"What does this have to do with me? And my quest to uncover my buried memories? And who the living hell are you?"

"Living Hell? How fitting for a demon yet to be born." The eyes blazed brighter as if someone just added another log to stoke the fire.

"Come out!" Lynx demanded.

"First, don't want to know how you were bitten?"

"I saw the memories – Claude bit part of my ear . . ." Lynx's trailed off. He flashed on the cub running away from his brother with half an ear, blood dripping -- no not dripping, streaming from the half that was left. His face crumbled, realizing his doesn't know what his true body is. And that is why Manx always wanted to fight him or acted as if he disliked him – calling him a phony once. A pretender. "I want to know what I am supposed to look like. I've asked for my soul to speak to me. To guide me or show me. I'm led in circles."

"Chasing your tail like a newborn cub," the voice taunted. "Are you ready?"

"Ready for what?" Lynx asked, digging a small hole at his feet, not sure he wanted to see.

The air thickened with humidity as dark clouds moved in and the wind pushed them away. The sun came out, but Lynx could feel the electricity building again –

The glowing eyes began to move forward at the same time the wind picked up, and abruptly the dark clouds covered the sun. The creature walked forward at a steady pace, as if counting the minutes. Thunder boomed. Everything went dark.

Lynx knew he had excellent eyesight at night – but he couldn't see through this. Lightning struck right in front of him, revealing a scrawny triangular face, with half of a right ear, crooked tail from being spun around so much as a cub and as the creature turned, as if on a catwalk, Lynx couldn't believe. There were horrible scars down his side where the fur wouldn't come back from being in a fire.

Chapter 20

Lynx woke up surrounded by Geoffrey, Soul Healer, Tarrier and Wayohm. Clarence was up on a shelf, looking down, just as worried.

"What happened?" Lynx asked. "Why are you all staring at me?"

"You shifted," Soul Healer said.

"What?"

"You faced something terrible," Soul Healer said.

Lynx shook his head, shrugging. Sitting up, trying to pull a paw up to lick it, he thought of Manx. "Where's Manx? And Artaois?"

"Gone," Soul Healer said. "After Artaois came out of his vision, he admitted you already had a soul. He couldn't give you a new one. But he said something with glowing eyes attacked his spirit self and whisked you away. What was left as a part of himself that knew what his parents were teaching him was a lie. Artaois felt defeated. When he saw you still lying there unconscious, he was concerned he killed you. Manx took him to see Albagoth."

Lynx looked at his paw again – his fur was bright orange with black stripes and his paws were narrow. But he still had thumbs. Maybe he always had thumbs. He snapped them. But couldn't get anything to happen.

Lifting a paw to his right ear, he felt it – part of it was gone. "What happened to my ear?"

"Claude bit it off," Soul Healer said. "You ran away before we could mend it. Claude was punished and almost excommunicated. But we allowed him to do his fire initiation first, early – and another soul was born in him. We didn't know what to do. We knew if he didn't accept the new soul, he would become that which is only in legends. Demon werecats used to walk the earth, fighting those they thought were weak or challenging the strong and attacking the Ohanaians – or humans, I've learned they are also called. All That Is has given various names for all of their creations on every world."

Lynx nodded, knowing it is true.

He twisted around to see his side – a large bare spot from his spine on down was there. He saw the burn marks and healed blisters. "My side!"

Tarrier smiled humbly, "I tried to heal you so the fur would grow back. When the villagers here saw your state, they either ran away in fear of you or felt sorry for you. I learned enough about werecats that I could trigger your shifting. So, I found what body that you would be most comfortable in and that wouldn't scare the villagers." Tarrier looked at Soul Healer and the others. "I'm sorry that I interfered with your pride. I was young and wanted to care for that young, injured werecat. I knew better – but felt the rules didn't apply to me. I learned different. I lost my chosen life of traveling to other worlds teaching, sharing and learning from them. I forgot to learn from you all."

"Tarrier, you learned a lesson. We did, too. We learned not to ignore a violent cub like we did with Claude. We needed to address his bullying sooner. Everything in life is lessons. Lessons the soul uses for our next time around," Soul Healer said.

Geoffrey smiled, "You remind me of my grandsire. He would have said that, too. Maybe in different words."

"We all learn from All That Is. And I suspect your grandsire was very close to All That Is and learned from their failures, like I did. They were harsh lessons." Soul Healer turned to Tarrier, the alchemist blacksmith. "You think Albagoth is angry with you for doing what you did. You can't forgive yourself. Therefore, you think Albagoth can't forgive you, too, isn't that right?"

Tarrier looked him, taken aback. "Yes, how did you know?"

"I catch glimpses of what is holding certain students back. I see yours so clearly. Especially as you look at Lynx's true form. You still feel guilty. Forgive yourself. And remove the block so Lynx will be able to access all his young memories," Soul Healer advised.

Tarrier nodded his head in understanding. Glancing at Lynx, he saw the werecat had a puzzled expression in his eyes.

"I'm sorry I did what I did, Lynx. I shouldn't have bothered you."

"But you saved me from the fire that Artaois threw at me, setting the wood pile and me on fire."

"Yes and no. There was a chance you would have found your way to survive the fire and found the strength within yourself to get out of there yourself. We never would know now what might have happened."

Tarrier visualized the blocks and the words came back to him. He began to process of removing the locks. Lynx moved, feeling suddenly antsy.

"Hold still," Soul Healer said.

"I got to move. I hear buzzing like there are thousands of bees around me," Lynx said.

"Hold still and relax. You're feeling the effects of the magic and enchantments," Soul Healer explained.

Lynx calmed himself, hearing the words, *Peace* within his mind. *Open, remember. Accept without judgment nor fear. Embrace and excel. Rise.*

Lynx heard an audible snap, like a padlock being released. In flooded memories of his Mamma and Dadpa looking at him with love as he frolicked with his weremates. He remembered a younger Soul Healer and an Ohanaian who was assisting them with the elderly werecats and those cubs were sick. He also remembered Claude when Claude wasn't a bully – but also remembered a crazed gleam in Claude's eyes, like he just had to tear something up. He trembled as he remembered Claude teasing and angrily abusing one of the females around, upset that she gets to care for the cubs and be mated. He wanted to do her job and have the male attention.

He remembered Dadpa telling him to crush the demon part and learn to shift. He remembered Claude learning his lessons as he prepared for his initiation ritual.

Then came the fateful day that he crossed Claude's demon side by wanting to eat. He remembered not getting enough to eat and others taking his food. He heard Claude say, "Starve the weak runt. He's taking up too much space and getting all the attention. Instead, Lynx remembered he fought Claude. He didn't like what he heard, so he attacked his older brother. He knew he had a right to live. But then Claude threw him against the cave wall. He smacked his head into the All That Is symbol and heard a voice say, "Save yourself, Runt. You are no longer Runt, but a Phoenix who will rise from the ashes. Run, and receive a new name."

When he got up, Lynx couldn't run out. Claude grabbed him, pushed him down and bite off part of his ear. He tried to fight back, instead, couldn't get his short legs to reach his brother's throat. All he could do was whimper in pain and panic. When Claude let go, he scampered to his feet and ran. Claude taunted him as he left, laughing and mocking him.

Lost, Lynx didn't know where to go. He knew the Ohanaian healer would be in the village, so he headed there. He needed a safe place to be.

But the bear family spotted him. Soon the younger bear cub broke off his family, disobeying and followed him. Spotting two Ohanaians he hadn't seen before, Lynx decided to go up to them to get attention, but the bear cub, who was older and larger, grabbed him, it was then that Lynx realized the bear's paws were on fire. The bear was speaking to him, but he couldn't understand the words. The cub's voice was deep and gravely. The bear threw him, after he touched his fur with one of his fire paws, so Lynx became a ball of fire and he landed in a wood pile at the bottom of wagon that was up on its side. Once Lynx remembered hitting the back of the wagon and it fell on top of him.

Lynx called for help – but couldn't form words. In the blaze, Lynx saw another werecat, "I am he who you will become. Accept your early initiation, little brother. Choose a name. Or choose to become the demon, like your brother, Claude. Roam this land hunting those that hurt you, with gleaming eyes of flames and terrorize this land."

Lynx remembered saying no to the vision. He refused to be like his brother. "I'm no demon. I'm too young. No demon."

"Walk out of here, little brother. Be the wise one. Face down the demon within you. Face down and survive. Or burn in your own fire of hell."

Before the runt could walk out, he heard Ohanaians speaking, yelling for water and more water as they rushed to put the inferno out before it spread to the stores nearby. Soon the fire was out, and the men were busy throwing off the wagon, what was left of it and then hands pulled him out.

He remembered Tarrier's gentle, grey eyes with blue flecks in them looking at him with love and care. Tarrier and another fellow washing his wounds and putting burn salve on them. Tarrier took him to another world, where he was taught to shift into a tabby cat. A Black and grey cat with the name Lynx. He remembered the new world had more Ohanaians – only there they were called humans, and they had other human like beings with one eye and dragons and walking, talking plants. Then he met teens from a new world called Nampa and that world wasn't supervised by crow judges, like Curá.

Hmm, Crow Judges. Lynx opened his eyes.

"I can't stay here. If the crow judges know I am in the area, they will be upset and exile me from Kent."

"No, they won't, Lynx," Tarrier re-assured. "I will tell them you are here for healing."

"Okay . . ." Lynx twisted around to look at his new shape and body. He sighed. "I'm no longer a Maine Coon."

"You are still you," Geoffrey said. "It is what you are in the inside that counts."

"Yeah, right. Spoken like you are ignoring how ugly I am."

Clarence said, "Not ugly. You've been through hell and survived."

"I still need to finish my initiation," Lynx said. "I want to do that at home. First, I need to go to the Reflection Pond."

Chapter 21

Lynx stood by the edge of the Reflection Pond. It hadn't changed much in the two or three years since he had been gone.

The water rippled with the light breeze across the Senilona desert. The Day Orb shone bright, turning and with each rotation, the color changed from a bright yellow to dim orange and to vibrate green and back to the bright yellow and so on. Lynx felt the warmth of the rays welcoming him home. He put a paw on his leg, still unaccustomed to his orange and black stripes, and not sure that was really his leg. But it had to be.

"Hey, Higher Self, are you in there?" Lynx called.

A Reflection of himself came into view, the same scared face, with half a right ear and triangular face with ears and long tuffs on the top of them.

"Hello. I'm glad to see you, Lynx. What do you want to know?" said the reflection.

Lynx cocked his head, puzzled, "Aren't you supposed to look older than me?"

"That isn't what you want to know. But yes, I am. Instead, I am showing you the face you need to see to reassure you of your true shape and body."

Lynx's eyes filled with water, as a lump rose to his throat. Taking a big breath and looking down, he swallowed and then took another big breath and let it out slow, then spoke, "If you always knew what my true body was, why didn't you tell me?"

"You weren't ready to face yourself, Lynx. Your memories were blocked. I saw through the blocks, but knew you weren't ready to see the truth. You are now. You can go home now. Home to your birth home."

"My home is with Xander and Milo," Lynx said.

"You choose that home, Lynx. It is your birth home you need to return to do. Your next step is to go through the fire ritual to set the soul on who you truly want to be. Demon or not. Until then, the demon will always taunt you. Haunting you."

Lynx shook his head, replaying all he had been through in the last few days. He was exhausted. Looking at himself, it was still strange to see himself as a bright orange with black stripes. He felt different, yet the same. Remembering the cub in his visions, the runt he used to be, was also this same color. And then he remembered Artaois almost tore his throat out.

He touched his throat. The wound wasn't there. Neither was the wound where Artaois ripped part of his back apart, taking him down. Puzzled he asked, "What happened to my wounds?"

The Reflection smiled, "Your present form heals fast because you are fully grown. But the scars from before your adulthood remain to remind you what you went through. Surviving your brother's assaults were worse for you, because he would become full demon. But he shares a body with another soul who is not. You will see when you meet him again."

"How do you know so much?"

"I am your Higher Self, who has access to your life records –your soul records for this life and many past lives. Lynx, you are the same werecat, in most ways. But you will also be very different from now on."

Lynx nodded, and hung his head, "Will the gang accept me when I get back to the World of Nampa?"

"They will love you, Lynx. You are their friend and companion. They may be shocked at first, but they will accept you."

A Flutter of wings and voices drew Lynx's attention away.

"We have company, Lynx. Face your fate."

Lynx turned to see Superior Court Crow Judges Sophia and Connor was also with her.

"Greetings, stranger, are you just visiting our world for the first time?" Crow Judge Sophia asked.

Another flutter of wings and voices drew their attention over toward the trees. They watched as Geoffrey landed with Clarence and Wayohm. Geoffrey held himself back, holding his breath, hoping the crow judges didn't arrest Lynx. Clarence and the river otter wanted to rush forward, but Geoffrey also held them back, explaining in a hush tone who the two black birds were and their status in this world.

Lynx looked back at the crow judges, "Hello, Crow Judges Connor and Sophia," he glanced down, humble.

Both flinched. "Do we know you?" Superior Crow Court Judge Connor asked, turning his head to one side and looking at him closer.

Crow Court Judge Sophia did the same, then smiled, "Yes, we do know him." Since she is the crow judge of wisdom, she saw through to his soul. "This is Lynx, Connor."

"No, it isn't. Lynx isn't devilish," Connor objected. Moving forward, he looked into Lynx's golden eyes, "We don't welcome creatures like you in Curá. You look like trouble. Answer our questions or we will banish you!"

"I'm just visiting, Superior Court Judges. I don't mean any trouble. I just needed to consult with the Reflection Pond," Lynx winced, lowering his head, not wanting to cause problems. He sighed as quietly as he could.

The Crow Judges exchanged looks. Connor grumbled, "Look, woman! Don't bother correcting me! I've been a Crow Judge before you were ever hatched!"

"Why the long face, Lynx?" Crow Judge Sophia asked, approaching him slowly.

Lynx backed away, "Don't come any closer to me, Crow Judge Sophia. I'm not here to hurt you all. I just want to finish my soul searching."

"Crow Judge Sophia! I'm your supervisor! Listen to me! That isn't Lynx! It's a demon for all we know! And it is resisting us!"

"Respectfully, Superior Crow Court Judge Connor, can it!" Geoffrey approached him.

"What did you say, Geoffrey, grandson of Healer Astral?" Crow Judge Connor turned to him, flapping his wings.

"Can it! That is Lynx! He knows he isn't supposed to be here, he is on a quest to understand what he missed. Alchemist Tarrier suppressed his memories and Lynx is now getting them back. He is in his rightful body."

"Rightful body?" Superior Crow Court Judge Connor spat. "What do you mean? That werecat knew he wasn't supposed to change shape! He was forbidden!"

"By whom?" Lynx growled, approaching the former spiritual overseer of this world. "No one forbade me to shift shape before I stole those damn keys to the Shadowlands! But the villagers of Kent objected to me having thumbs once Tarrier triggered my ability to create them!" he snarled. "And I dare remind you, Crow Judge Connor, Sophia is the new overseer in this world! You may still be teaching her the ropes, but she sees the truth deep within a person! I am no common critter! And certainly, I am no demon!"

"We shall see about that!" Superior Crow Court Judge Connor raised his wings getting ready to pronounce judgment. Before he could, Lynx acted.

"Smite!" Lynx snapped his thumbs, rendering Crow Judge Connor incapable of talking or moving.

Lynx's friends gasped, "Lynx, what did you do?"

Lynx lowered his paw and shook his head and body. Slowly, he approached the frozen crow judge, sniffing and carefully examining him. He shrugged.

"I don't know what I did. I hope I didn't kill him. I was angry that he called me a demon. . ."

Sophia approached him, "Lynx, you aren't used to your new shape. This shape comes with new abilities that will happen before you understand them."

"But they aren't set yet. I haven't had my proper fire initiation, Crow Judge Sophia. I'm no demon."

"I know this. You are still a kitten in this form," she replied.

"Tarrier won't be punished for what he did, will he?" Lynx said.

"No. He has punished himself. He and I have had many talks after you left with Geoffrey and the Indigo Travelers," she re-assured. "Are they with you?"

"No, Wayohm, the river otter over there and I left without them. We didn't want the teens to follow us," Lynx admitted.

"I understand. This was your quest, as Geoffrey said." She looked at Geoffrey. "Thank you for vouching for Lynx."

"It is my pleasure. I must look out for him. He's my buddy," Geoffrey said.

"Mine, too," Clarence chimed in, strolling forward with his head held high and swaying his tail and body, with pride and pomposity.

Crow Court Judge Sophia nodded, and then looked at the river otter.

Not to be out done, Wayohm scampered forward. "He's my friend, too. Though I couldn't fight Artaois much. I still want to protect Lynx. He's a good werecat and wouldn't hurt anyone on purpose." The river otter glanced at the frozen crow judge, "He isn't hurt, is he?"

"No, he can be unfrozen," Sophia turned to Lynx, "Being you are here to on a quest, you aren't to be punished. I understand you will be leaving when you are done." She paused, and those watching could tell she was listening to a voice deep within her. She nodded. "I have just been told you are forgiven for what you did three years ago. You have shown valor in protecting Sarah in Wayla and making sure everyone got back to the World of Nampa safely. You have suffered quite bit with this misguided bear who was raised to believe he is a god. Albagoth has dealt with him. Snap your thumbs to release Connor." Lynx did.

Superior Crow Court Judge fell forward, caught himself, ruffled his feathers and shook himself. Taking a deep breath, he glanced around. He puffed out his chest and then noticed Lynx standing with his head held high, and the crow judge deflated his chest as he realized he was in the wrong.

"I'm sorry, Lynx. I misjudged you. I didn't recognize you and I'm in the wrong."

"You heard it all?" Lynx asked looking suspiciously.

"Yes, I could hear it all. While I was listening to you, Albagoth and my superiors were filling me in on what else has been taking place. I spoke out of turn."

"You're forgiven, Superior Crow Court Judge, Connor.

Chapter 22

Back on Ohana, Lynx roamed the area, investigating places he didn't have time to see before. Sniffing the flowers and the trees and pausing to consider how different this world was from the other ones he had been to.

The flowers, yellow leaves and green petals, smelled like lemons and other flowers with a light yellow that reminded him of urine, smelled more like vinegar. The blue flowers, by a stream not far off from the werecat pride, reminded him of blueberries and huckleberries that he found up in the mountains where the Veh's go camping every summer.

The air smelled fresh, like after a good rain. Lynx inhaled deeply, closing his eyes to savor the wonderful aroma, and taking delight in the sound of the bees and birds going about their own activities. Despite being a different color and having his wounds showing, Lynx was grateful for being alive.

He heard someone approaching, so he opened his eyes to see the Ohanaian boy that was apprenticed to Soul Healer walking to him.

"Soul Healer says they are ready for you. Are you ready for your initiation?" the boy said.

"Not sure if I will ever be ready," Lynx answered and pawed the ground, suddenly aware of why he was spending so much time away from the cave. He wanted to forget the ritual. Looking up, "I will never be ready, but I must do this to finish this process so I can get back to my home."

Lynx walked next to the boy, noticing his ears were lengthening and fur orange and black fur was growing on his face, arms and head. Lynx remembered Soul Healer saying his mom was raped by a werecat. Or mated with one but didn't say who.

"What was your name?" Lynx asked.

"I haven't been named. But back in the village, they call me Demonson because my father was a demon werecat. He attacked my mom. Others say she willingly laid with him, but I know different."

"Demonson. Hmm, I would change my name. You aren't a demon. Give yourself a name that you like," Lynx suggested.

"Salem. I like the name Salem. Not sure why. I think it is a good name for a healer. I have heard it in my visions of the All That Is. I hear them telling me to embrace the past while molding it to become something totally different." Salem looked at Lynx and smiled. "You fear the flames. But the flames won't consume you. You are too strong for them. In the flames, you will see your fears and meet yourself once more, be taunted with becoming or owning the demon. My father bit you when you were called runt. You are no longer that runt and no longer afraid of your own shadow. Stand tall and become what you want to be."

Salem's words lightened Lynx's spirit, inspiring him. Still he didn't know what to expect.

"Spoken like an old soul," Lynx replied. But he changed the topic. "Do you ever see your father?"

"Not always. My father chooses his second self. But since you have been gone, he has been sulking around, glad Soul Healer isn't around. His second self has to care for the cubs and he despises that because he had to do it when he was younger. He is the one that scared you off and hurt you. Didn't you see him when you all returned the other day?"

Lynx shook his head, "I was tired and just wanted to curl up and sleep. But I had visions of Claude . . ." he gasped.

"Where is Lyraca?" Lynx said. "Claude is your father?"

"Yes. Lyraca is my father's second self" Salem replied.

Lynx gasped, "I was falling in love with my brother! Oh, my Albagoth!"

"Soul Healer told you she wasn't who you thought she was and cautioned you to be careful of how your attractions were to her."

Lynx observed the fire in the center of a rectangular stone barrier. He guessed it was about six feet or more long and about 8 feet wide. *It can't be that bad*, Lynx mused to himself. *All I must do is walk across that and survive.*

Soul Healer came up to him. Lynx heard the other werecats approaching along with his friends, Geoffrey, Clarence, Wayohm and Manx. Seeing them in the crowd was comforting. Salem stood with the Ohanaians who choose to come so they could beat the drums in time, with those of the trained Werecats whom assist with vision quests in the pride and rituals. The crowd all talked at once, in their own private conversations. All Lynx could hear were the murmuring of the voices, but he couldn't make out individual words or subjects. He guessed they were making bets on what Lynx would choose once in the fire.

Spotting Claude in the audience deflated Lynx a bit, because he could feel his brother taunts, urging him to become the demon, too. Claude wanted another demon among the pride.

Not going to happen, Claude, Lynx thought to himself, but could feel his lips moving with his words. He hoped he didn't say it loud enough for all to hear it.

Soul Healer, standing on his back paws, raised his staff in the air, quieting the crowd. Once all the voices were silenced, he turned to Lynx.

"You know what do, right?"

"Walk through the fire and out the other side. Xander has told me about fire walks the humans do in his world to help them gain confidence in themselves. They walk across without shoes and expecting not to burn their feet. Most don't. But those that fear, usually do. I guess this will be like that. It shouldn't take that long."

Soul Healer smiled in such a way that made Lynx's fur crawl and slightly raise. He felt like a little cub once again.

"I'm not even close, am I?"

"Lynx, you haven't been listening to my instructions. This is your coming of age initiation. Inside these flames, you will meet yourself. We will be faced with many selves. It is your chance to see and choose who you will be. I cannot say whom you will be meet. But they will be scary. Remember, the demon werecat bit you when you were a runt, before Claude knew he was already going with the demon. But he also accepted another soul to enter his body. They now fight for who will control his body. To some extent, he can choose who has the control. Some cannot choose that."

Lynx thought about it. "I'm not a demon. I don't lose control of myself nor have I showed a tendency to beat people less than me up. That isn't who I am."

"The demon isn't always about hurting others. Sometimes it is about accepting the temptations to do what you know is wrong. Stealing keys to a forbidden world . . ."

"But Tarrier was in trouble and falsely accused . . ."

Soul Healer wagged a toe at him, "Maybe so, but there might have been another way to prove his innocence."

"We will never know now," Lynx said. "It's over and done with and the Superior Crow Court forgave me."

"In the past, that is." Soul Healer bowed his head, "Take a few moments to prepare yourself."

Lynx closed his amber eyes, directing his thoughts to Albagoth. A voice boomed in answer *Direct your soul to come to be with you. It is your soul you need to meet once more. It takes many forms, for you have had many lives, Lynx. Seek the soul for whom you need to be and which purpose resonates with you. It is your choice. Create your own life. Not the life others may want for you.*

The voice was gone.

Lynx nodded. *Soul, I beckon you once more to guide me. Please meet me in the fire.* As soon as he had thought that, he felt someone Gib smack him as if it say that was a dumb thing to say. *Thank you, Captain Obvious.*

Lynx squeezed his closed eyes, hoping to let go of the awful stupid feeling that descended on him. He knew he needed to clear his mind to focus on his intent. *Soul – True self- assist me.*

Soul Healer smiled and nodded. "The pupil is ready," he stated proudly. "Add more wood and incense." Salem and other attendants brought the incense and wood and then jumped back as the fire spat sparks and bits of burned wood out as it began to grow up and out the length of the boundaries.

Lynx winced, trying to calm his shaking legs.

Soul Healer directed the drummers to begin their rhythmic beat and chant. Lynx felt his inner being resonating with beat.

"Begin your walk, Lynx."

Lynx turned to Soul Healer with a mischievous twinkle in his eyes, "What? No fancy mumble jumble about what I am about to face?"

Soul Healer's eyes flashed red flames that at first, Lynx took for the reflection of the fires he was about to enter, "You want fancy mumble jumble! Fancy this," he answered, raising his staff high in the air, and reaching deep within his abdomen, he boomed, "All That Is, bring forth the Demon Werecat to taunt Lynx- show him the many selves he needs to encounter—send him to the gates of a deep pit to tangle with the most horrible werecat demons ever! May his Soul either guide him to the right Soul/Spirit that is his for this life, or may he be devoured by the demon and forced to roam all worlds lusting for terror of all beings he encounters! May All That Is rest in this ritual!"

Lynx's hunches rose as his flight or fight instincts took over.

"I can't do this. I can't do this. I can't face that fire again. Once in a lifetime is enough."

All at once, a familiar yet fearsome voice spoke above the drums, "You can do this, Lynx! If you don't, I will personally march you through those flames again!"

Lynx turned to see Artaois strolling to the forefront. His heart raced, his legs trembled, and the bear frightened him for the first time since he was a cub. Lynx bolted into the fire without thinking.

Straight in and straight out. Straight out, Lynx chanted to himself. *It won't take long. Nothing will happen. I won't encounter anything. No werecat demon will meet me in here. I don't have anything to be afraid of except fear itself. What I visualize will manifest if I keep a clear mind.*

His mind flashed on Claude, taunting him when Salem and him first got back to the Pride cave, "You're nothing but a runt, Runt! I bit you! I marked you! I left the demon mark on you. You have no choice in that fire, but the demon you are meant to be! Just because you haven't shown any signs of it, doesn't mean you can escape it! I'm a demon! You will be, too!"

"You have another soul within you," Lynx recalled saying. "Lyraca is there somewhere. You choose whom to show."

"Lyraca is weak!" Claude snarled. "I will kill that female off!" Suddenly Claude fell to the ground, withering as if another werecat pounced on him.

Gradually, he saw Claude shift from muscular and scar ridden to trim, confident and calm Lyraca.

"Don't listen to Claude," she said. "I won't ever allow Claude to hurt you again, Lynx. You can fight the demon if it approaches you. You know what to do."

"Will I become two souled, too?" Lynx asked.

"No need to. But no one knows for sure what you will encounter in that fire. It is different for each individual werecat," Lyraca said. "Go, they are waiting for you."

The flames licked at his whiskers, and the embers signed his pads, bringing his attention back to the present moment.

"Right, be here now!" he said out loud.

What he thought would be a straight in, straight out fire walk stretched into a thousand-mile walk. When he reached what he thought was the center, a doorway opened, causing Lynx to stop and ponder. He saw two hallways.

"Come in, Lynx," a voice called through one doorway. The voice sounded oddly like him.

Manic laughter assaulted him from the other door. "Choose this door," another voice called. "Meet the self you are supposed to be here."

Lynx lifted a foot and scratched his chin, considering. "What if I don't choose either of these doors? Besides, there is no doorway in the fire."

"The ritual fire is magical, Lynx. What you see before you enter is not what you encounter. You need to choose one of these doors. If you choose to go around this, we will still confront you," advised the voice from the right door.

The manic laughter grew louder from the left door. It sounded like there were more than one creature in there.

Maybe it's a party. Lynx decided to choose that door. As he crossed the threshold, the doors morphed into one. Lynx faced two versions of himself – one with the same orange and black stripes, with a triangular face like he had now and there was a majestic Maine Coon, head held high, tail regally held high, like a flag that said no one could mess with him.

Lynx shook his head, squeezing his eyes shut, *I must be hallucinating.*

"No, you aren't. We are you, but we are not you," the two Lynxes said in unison.

"What? How can you be me but not me?"

The demon Lynx stepped forward, his eyes blazing, his ear tufts growing into horns, and long saber teeth coming down from his upper maw.

"I am the demon – the one that will haunt you, pounce on others and terrorize those who would never hurt you. Evil – you are pure evil. You want to be me. I know you do."

He flashed his eyes, lifting a paw, snapping his thumbs against the first toe, lightning struck. Thunder boomed. Instantly, Lynx, the true Lynx, felt himself transform into a fiery, angry filled instead, longing to tear apart Tarrier for what he did to him. "I can't forgive you for taking away who I am! How dare you play creator with my life! You robbed me! I will make you pay!"

Lynx saw himself chasing down his old friend and caretaker, pouncing on him and ripping him apart, lusting for blood and eager to hurt anyone who crossed his path.

Next, he saw himself ripping the crow court judges apart for punishing him for taking the keys to Shadowlands. Feathers spraying all over, loose and floating haphazardly around him. "I will never obey anyone that forces me to become what I am not! I am not your puppet!"

Next, he saw himself chasing down Claude and tearing into him for how Claude treated him as a cub. "I'm no longer your punching bag! You gave me this demon bite! I will destroy you and any of your offspring!"

Suddenly, Salem was there in front of him, "This isn't you, Lynx. There is another choice." Lynx stopped short. He locked deep into Salem's eyes, large, golden eyes, filled of love, hope and honesty. His heart melted, shaking off the deep soul, he said, "I refuse to be that creature! I am no demon!"

The Maine Coon strolled forward, "Would you rather be me? Full of mischief, willing to pull pranks on your friends, and sharing midnight talks with Erin?"

Lynx stepped into that soul, felt love spreading throughout his body, saw himself sitting up with Erin, Xander's Mom, under the moonlight, talking about the day, the boys and Sarah and Mark's work. Erin, with her soft brown eyes, enjoying cooking and caring for Geoffrey, Clarence and himself. And Lynx doing what he can to assist Erin to relax and not worry so much about the kids and their travels to other worlds.

"This is who I want to be," Lynx said. "This is who I am. I am not demon. Claude did bite me, but I don't choose the demon."

"Demon is always present with you, Lynx. Demons are born in fire. Fire of Claude's anger. There will come a day, that the dormant demon disease will surface and take over," taunted the demon Lynx.

"And that will not happen, if I can help it!" Lynx replied.

"You can't say that. You won't be able to prevent it. Your will doesn't belong to you," The Demon Lynx snarled, raising a paw in the air. The paw opened. His face grew dark, his eyes narrowed. Curling his toes in, he boomed, "Your will is mine! Once a demon always a demon!"

Abruptly, something took hold of Lynx, twisting and contorting his being and Lynx fought it off, yet whatever it was it held him from untangling himself. "Soul, my true soul, come forward and assist me to fight this!"

"In the name of Albagoth, Release me!" The words rushed out of his mouth, sounding like they were coming from above and not inside him. The demon self let go. Lynx snarled, growled and hissed as he rushed forward and pounced on the demon self. They rolled and clawed each other.

"I am much stronger than you are!" The demon said. "We are one. You want to be filled with anger all the time. You need the anger to feel alive and fight all who cross you. Never will you want to be the milk toast sap again!"

"Never! Never will I submit to this. I will destroy you!" Lynx roared. Lynx latched his jaws onto the

Demon's jugular vein and bite down as hard as he could. The demon cried out, bringing his front paws up and raked his razor-sharp claws down his face to distract him. The ground rumbled, tremored as a loud pop echoed through the fire. The firm rock underneath them opened and they fell through it.

As Lynx descended, head over tail, he twisted himself to get his feet below him. It then occurred to him, Claude did bite him, but the demon fire within him isn't because of Claude. It was something else fueling this. He had to figure it out.

"I am not Claude!" he shouted. "Claude did not make me!"

They landed the center of The Land. Molten lava ran down the sides of the cavern and then the two werecat selves broke apart.

"Hello, down there! Are you two alright?" called the Maine Coon self. The other two looked up.

"No, stupid! We fell 20 feet to our death! It's our ghosts you are looking at asshat!" snarled the demon self.

Lynx snarled at him, "Can't you be nice?"

"He asked a stupid question and deserves a sarcastic answer to remember how dumb he is. Besides, it isn't in my nature. Nor is it supposed to be in yours to be such a stupid milk toast, goody-four-feet!"

Lynx hissed at him. Then looking up, he made eye contact with his other self, "We're fine. It's too bad fall didn't kill the demon, though."

The Maine Coon self laughed. "I'm coming down." Lifting his right paw, he snapped his toe and thumb and transported down.

"Now what do we do?" Lynx said, looking from one of his selves to the other.

The Maine Coon smiled, shrugging, "We go forward down the trail and see what else is in store."

"I thought this ritual would be straight across the fire and out the other side. But this is longer than I thought," Lynx said. "What else will I encounter?"

"You will encounter many trials. We are not the only ones," said the pleasant self. "You must choose who you want to be."

"But I am whom I am. It's been three years. Why now?"

"Because you weren't ready. Your memories and ability to see and recognize us was blocked. There are legends which demonize us werecats. Based on fact and myth. Sometimes the truth is simple and sometimes the truth is more bizarre. Without encountering us, you would not understand or have a set shape/soul to be comfortable being when you shed your Maine Coon image. Deep down you fear fire. Deep down, you are drawn to fire. Deep down, Claude's taunts haunt you. You want to lash out but restrain yourself. When is it okay to fight? When you choose to fight, you release the demon. When is it okay to walk away from a threatening animal, person or situation? You are not always chicken to walk away. And it is not always bad to fight."

Lynx felt conflicted. "I have to think on that." They walked in silence. "I don't remember being so conflicted."

They came to a deep gorge. They could feel hear the inferno snapping, crackling and sparks jumped up to singe their whiskers.

"Remember when Artaois attacked you and Lyraca? You didn't want to fight. You were afraid to fight. It was your life at stake. Lyraca quickly shifted to Claude so he could fight the bear. But you withdrew in fright, until the bear threw Claude aside and attacked you and even then, you barely harmed him. Artaois came close to killing us."

"Numbskull! You need me!" Demon Lynx said. "I will fight for you! You need me!"

Lynx's heart sunk deep within him. "It goes against my teachings. I am, I'm not supposed to hurt anyone."

"Protect yourself! Lynx, you must fight to protect yourself when attacked. Otherwise others will walk or run right over you!" Demon Lynx chastised.

"No – No—No! I can't allow myself to be swallowed up in your hate!"

"Hate? You think all I am is hatred and anger and seeking to punish others? You have no idea who I am!"

"I don't know what to do." Lynx said, trembling staring down in the deep gorge before them.

"Jump!" Maine Coon's gentle prompting directed him.

Lynx backed up and took a running leap and made it across the gorge. The others followed.

"There is no easy way out," said the demon. "You must choose."

Lynx sped up trying to get ahead of the other two. Finding a reflective wall up ahead, Lynx walked past it, glancing at it expecting to see the other two selves walking behind, but he was the only one. Lynx did a double take, and then turned around and came back to stand. He sat and examined it, puzzled.

"Why aren't you two reflected in this mirror rock?" Lynx asked.

"Because we are inside of you, Lynx. You cannot kill what is already part of you. You control what you are. You choose to be the body and persona you want to be," said the Maine Coon.

"If I choose to be my birth shape, does that mean I am choosing to be full demon?" Lynx asked.

"No, you can be your birth body/shape and not be demon. Only be demon when you need to defend yourself."

"I am sweet, calm, mischievous and loving," Lynx said. "This is who I want to be." Sitting down, he sighed. "But will Xander and the kids accept me in this body?"

"They will see the good heart and soul you have deep within you. They will love you no matter what," said the Maine Coon. "And when you want to, you can shift into the Maine Coon when the kids' friends come over. They will also accept you."

As Lynx walked past the reflected rock wall, he saw his other shapes and a small cub walking in behind him. While in midair, he announced,

"I am ready," Lynx said. "I accept myself. Pure, white, loving white light. I go with the grace of Albagoth." All three selves merged within Lynx as he landed near the edge of the fire. He stood, turned and walked out of the fire into the cold evening.

Looking around, Lynx wondered where everyone was. The drums still beat, and torches were lite. Then a cheering rose from the bystanders. Geoffrey, Clarence and Wayohm rushed out and hugged him.

"Now, we feast!" Soul Healer announced.

Chapter 23

Lynx looked at all the food that was laid out. Ohanaians from the village he didn't have a chance to meet or talk with even came. He noticed a woman with long hair that was black and sprinkled with natural grey highlights was standing by herself under a tree. Perking up his ears, he wondered who she was and why she wasn't mixing with the others. Geoffrey walked up to him.

"We were worried you wouldn't come out. You were in there for a very long time," Geoffrey said. "What happened?"

Lynx shrugged. "It's hard to say. It's something I want to talk with Soul Healer about."

Geoffrey prodded him, "Come on, you can tell me."

"Geoffrey, I haven't processed it all. There are many layers to what I experienced. I thought it would still be daylight when I came out. The time is different inside that ritual fire."

Claude came up next. Lynx narrowed his eyes, growled lowly and raised his hackles.

"Well, Runt, you lived. You shocked me. That bear god didn't devour you. You survived his fire and you survived this. You're tougher than I thought you would be. I expected you to die as cub. I really expected it. Maybe you survived despite you being as dumb as weed."

"Shut that big fricken mouth of yours Claude!" Lynx snarled, picking up a paw, unsheathing his claws and swiping his brother across the face. "Stay away from me!"

Claude tumbled head over tail. When he stopped rolling, he picked himself, put a paw to his face, wiping the blood and pain. "Why did you do that, Runt? I was just saying . . ."

"Stop calling me Runt! I'm no longer a runt and I will not allow you to treat me like your punching bag anymore! If you can't respect me, then leave me fricken alone!" Lynx roared.

Once the area was full of everyone talking at once, but now it was a still as Veh house at midnight. Then everyone around him cheered and clapped their hands or paws. Even the woman who stood alone. Lynx wasn't sure what he did, but being in the spotlight made him want to disappear. He noticed Salem was at Claude's side, whispering in his ear, and then Claude went away with his son. A moment later, Salem was over at the woman's side.

"Come on, Geoff, let's find Soul Healer and the others. I need to get some rest. I'm tired. I'm exhausted."

They didn't get that far when Salem stopped him. Next to him was the woman.

"Lynx, before you head into the cave to go over your experience with the ritual, I want you to meet my mom," Salem said.

"Hi, I want to say I admire you for standing up to your bully," the woman said. "I am Lyraca."

"You're Lyraca? How can that be?" Lynx said.

"I am not the one that Claude becomes. He attacked and raped me before he knew my name. When he went through his ritual, a piece of me ended up with him, but it took on a whole 'nother soul. It turns out, it wasn't truly me. While you and the others were in that other world, my healers were able to pin Claude down and pull out the soul, but discovered it really was a different soul. It just took on my name because she wanted to sing and be something it knew Claude could never be. The part of me that was within Claude was released and reunited with me. I am whole now. But Claude stays away from me."

"That's a good thing, right?" Lynx and Geoffrey said.

"Yes, it is. I don't like being around him. Sometimes just being with other werecats gives me flashbacks of being attacked. No one knows why Claude attacked me. He was in full demon mode. Not sure where it came from . . ."

"Legend has it a demon gene came into his system before he even opened his eyes as a cub," Salem said. "I heard a demon member of the pride choose Claude, since he was the first born, to bite and carry it on. Grandmamma said Claude had a fresh bite from someone and she doesn't know who did this. But Grandpappa took out the werecat member once he found out. No one has missed that member since."

Soul Healer approached, "Yes, that is true, Salem. Now, can you walk your momma to her home so she will get there safe?"

"Yes, Teacher," Salem bowed.

Soul Healer turned to Lynx, "It's time for us to talk about your experience. Come, Lynx. Follow me."

Lynx glanced around the small room off the main living area of the cave, noticing the Albagoth symbol on the wall, the smaller circle within the larger one and many lines or paths leading to the smaller one.

Settling down, he reflected on the memory of Claude slapping him so hard, he landed in the middle of it. It occurred to him that he'd felt a zap from the middle part. Sighing, he wondered if Albagoth if had been watching over him all this time, and he never knew it.

Cocking his head to one side, he wasn't sure what to make of that. Maybe it was possible. Only, in this world, Albagoth is called All That Is.

"All That Is watches over all individuals in Ohana. Even if that individual doesn't recognize them. Mostly, All That Is leads each individual within when they know they are ready. It's seldom that a bear is ever ready to acknowledge them, though. Artaois is the first one to meet All That Is face to face," Soul Healer said.

Lynx hung his head, still not used to the old healer knowing his thoughts. "So, hitting the center of that drawing didn't zap me?"

"Just hitting the wall was a slap, Lynx. All That Is used that to remind you not to be afraid. But you were too young to heed that sign. Still things worked out for you."

Lynx nodded. A helper came in with herbal tea, a small plate of biscuits and meat cubes. "But you didn't call me away to discuss this. You wanted me to tell you what I experienced in the fire?"

"Yes. Part of processing your ritual is to tell me what you saw and for you to ask questions."

Nodding, he let all that he experienced come rushing in. Squeezing his eyes shut, he focused on what was important.

"I saw two versions of myself. One was angry and wanted me to choose to be him all the time, taking revenge on all who have hurt me. He criticized me for not fighting Artaois when he attacked Lyraca and myself. The other one was my Maine Coon Self, gentle, loving and mischievous. The one who listens to my Clarence's staff when she can't sleep and is worried about her boys. They said I had to choose which one I wanted to be. But the trick is, they are both inside of me."

Lynx nibbled on a biscuit, wishing for Erin's homemade butter and cheese dipping sauce. "They also said the ritual isn't over. There will be more selves for me to meet. I expected to encounter more horrors, but nothing else came to me. Once I said I choose my birth shape, I was out of the fire."

"The ritual will come again on the next journey you take with one Indigo boy you don't know well. Remember the walking path you and the river otter came through?" Soul Healer said.

"Yes, I do. We need to get back home."

"Manx will be taking you all home. First, know this. One forlorn Indigo teen much younger than your friends is preparing to go through that portal and he needs your assistance. You must go with him. He will think no one else is watching him. You and he will face many obstacles that will frighten him and make him want to give up. Be the brave werecat, Lynx. Dare to be the demon for good, knowing not all demon werecats are like Claude."

"Ian Temple," Lynx mused, remembering back. "I warned Ian to stay away from it."

"He is desperate for change in his life. He wants to give up. His home life isn't what your wards have," Soul Healer advised.

Chapter 24

Geoffrey, Manx and Lynx saw Wayohm reunited
with his family and Artaois to his own den. Artaois
apologized for how he treated Lynx and the others.
He understood humans were not all bad and said he
would do his best to be the guardian of the forest
animals, instead of their god and controller of what
they do.

Clarence was left at home, where he let Xander and
Milo know they were home safe.

Xander, Milo and Sarah came out to welcome Lynx
and Geoffrey, but did a double take when they
noticed Lynx with his healed half an ear and large
scar down his left side with fur missing. His bright
orange and black also startled them.

"Orange and black, be very afraid," Sarah muttered.

Lynx perked his ears. "What's that, Sarah?"

"It is an old nursery rhyme. Orange and black is what
tigers are and they are very frightening wild cats. But
they don't have the fierce triangular face you have,"
Sarah explained.

"What happened?" Xander and Milo asked.

"This is how I am supposed to be. My ear was bitten
off by my brother Claude when I was a runt cub,"
Lynx pawed his ear. And then twisted around to show
the scar, "This is the scar from when that misguided
bear god set me on fire as a cub. Tarrier and Sage of
Stillness did rescue me, but Tarrier lost his
apprenticeship for interfering with the animal life on
Ohana."

"Ohana? That means family in Hawaiian language," Milo said.

"Ohana means The Land. I was born on Ohana, not Curá. I spent time with my pride mates and family. I faced the demon fires and rituals. I faced that bear and lived."

The teens smiled, exchanging glances and Lynx could tell they were processing it all. They smiled, laughed and then ran to him, embracing him.

"We love you, Lynx. We're glad you're back. And glad we know who you are," Xander said. The other two agreed.

Sarah broke away, "And your new appearance will be perfect for All Hallow's Eve. Which is this weekend."

All Hallow's Eve fell on a Saturday. Sarah and Nickoli spent all day at the Veh's house preparing. Xander choosing an all-cotton peasant style shirt, like what he wore in Curá and cotton trousers. He put his dragon's blood sword in a special harness and sheath and strapped it over his shoulders. Sarah dressed in her black trousers, and black peasant blouse with leather straps, silver buckles and knee-high platform boots. She looked more like a pirate buccaneer than a Murdoc warrior.

Milo dressed in a Shakespearean blouse with billowing sleeves and ruffles down the front, knickers and tights with a Musketeer's hat with a large feather in it. He carried a quill and scrolls in a leather satchel.

Sarah made her face up to look like she had many scars. Finally, she looked at Geoffrey and Lynx.

Sarah and Nickoli altered Geoffrey's glamour and sprayed him with washable sparkles so he glittered. They made it look like he was a Great Dane that appeared to be a griffin with fake wings. Lynx was fine with his new shape.

"Remember, Lynx, if you want to shift into your Maine Coon body, do. But this is All Hallow's Eve. This is a day to scare the bejeezus out of friends and enemies," Sarah said.

All five jumped in the truck. The kids in the cab and animals, (though Lynx and Geoffrey don't admit to being animals) in the truck bed.

Before they went into the school gym for the dance, Sarah put a glamour over Xander's sword, so it didn't look real. They called it a LARPing sword, made of foam and cord.

Before they even got inside, Betty, the one that flirts with Xander, approached them, dressed as a Disney princess, Snow White, fair and fragile.

"Oh, Xander, my handsome prince. You've come to save me!" She swooned.

Sarah reached over, drew Xander's sword, "Not in your life! Back, you fragile creature! before I separate your pretty little head from your pearly white shoulders!"

"Sarah be nice," Xander chided. "Betty, have you seen Geoffrey, my dog?" he asked, noticing her the rest of her clique approaching.

Geoffrey strolled up and tried to pant, and it wasn't a bad attempt.

"Eek! What's that?" Betty squealed seeing Lynx approaching, lips curled and hissing.

Lynx hissed, "Garrowl! I say, Grrowl!" he attempted to claw her with his sharp claws, trying to step into his demon self.

"What did you do your precious Maine Coon? He's a demon cat!" Betty turned around and ran away.

They looked at each other and laughed. Lynx giggled.

"She didn't even notice me," Geoffrey said.

But in the distance, Butch did. He knew Geoffrey was the griffin that he tried to steal four years ago. But he refused to say it.

Epilogue

It was a cold November night, everyone was asleep. Ian Temple knew the animals would be inside where it was warm.

"No one will notice me. I have nothing to live for and no one will miss me. This walking path is a mystery. Trees follow me wherever I go, and crows and griffins watch me, saying they are my guides and teachers. I must know why. That werecat said there is a portal in the middle. I'm so alone. No one understands me."

"You need to understand yourself," Lynx said in a deep voice, from a dark doghouse. He tried to disguise it so Ian wouldn't know.

Ian turned around but didn't see anything. Shuddering, he stepped forward and started on the walking path, crying and not expecting anything to happen. He remembered seeing the animals go through the portal a month ago. The moon was large, and still bright orange with pale clouds drifting by. The breeze chilled him to the bone. As he jumped on to the center stone, he felt something with rough pads and claws take his hand.

Coming soon:
Ian Temple and the Search for the Wisdom Trees
Working title

Made in the USA
Lexington, KY
15 December 2019

58602161R00156